"This well-written story helps us all understand the frustration and pain, the spiritual strength and the hope, of Native young people today...Highly recommended for young people and educators."
CASNP Resource Reading List

"Teenagers who want to know more about the real grievances of native Canadians will find some provocative and absorbing food for thought in this impressive first novel."
Children's Book News

"Recommended...a powerful story...The themes of suicide, grief, dignity and values are explored in this powerful novel."
Language Arts Resource List, B.C. Ministry of Education

WHERE THE RIVERS MEET

Don Sawyer

Cover Art by Gilbert Freynet. All rights reserved.

Cover Design by Jim Kirby

Pemmican Publications Inc. gratefully acknowledges the assistance accorded to its publishing program by Manitoba Arts Council and Canada Council.

Printed by Hignell Book Printing, Winnipeg, MB
Seventh Printing 2001

Canadian Cataloguing in Publication Data

Sawyer, Don, 1947-
    Where the rivers meet

    ISBN: 0-921827-06-7
I. Title.

PS8587.A89W5 1988   C813'.54   C89-098015-2
PR9199.3.S389W5 1988

**PEMMICAN
PUBLICATIONS
INC.**

150 Henry Avenue / Winnipeg, Manitoba / Canada R3B 0J7

DEDICATION

This book is dedicated to the memory of Adelarde Christian, Chuckie Peters, Bill Tomma and Charlee Edwards. May their deaths remind us of the pain that lies behind and the work that lies ahead.

ACKNOWLEDGEMENTS

I would particularly like to acknowledge the invaluable contributions of Shuswap elder Mary Thomas. Much of the spiritual content of the book is based on her experience and rich knowledge of Shuwap traditions, and I am deeply indebted to her for the hours of interviews and the wisdom and stories she so generously shared.

I would also like to acknowledge Mrs. Suzanne Swartz, Thompson elder, for her kindness and inspiration, and Tom Wayman for his advice and encouragement. There cannot be a more generous and supportive mentor.

Finally, I want to acknowledge the use of several secondary sources: James Teit's *The Thompson Indians of British Columbia* and *The Shuswap Indians of British Columbia* (New York: American Museum of Natural History, 1900), and *The Sacred*, edited by Peggy Beck and Anna Walters (Tsaile, Arizona: Navajo Community College Press, 1977).

A portion of the proceeds from this book will be donated to the Lytton and Mt. Currie Stein Preservation Fund, Box 1420, Lillooet, B.C., V0K 1V0, and the Stein Natural and Cultural Heritage Rediscovery Society, Lytton, B.C., V0K 1Z0.

Where the Rivers Meet

I.

The railroad trestle lay across the canyon like a web strung between two enormous rocks. Far below the wooden beams of the trestle, the gorge was choked with water boiling between the steep sides. A constant low roar climbed up the canyon walls. Jagged snow-tipped peaks rose on either side of the river like rows of gigantic wolves' teeth.

Nancy Antoine stood silently in the middle of the trestle. Her feet were planted on two ties and between them she could see the tangled river a thousand feet below her. She rocked toward the edge, catching her balance just before she swayed an inch too far and arched like a diving eagle to the rocks below. She liked the rush of excitement as she swayed forward until she could see the water beyond the dark brown edge of the railroad ties.

She studied the water as it boiled through the gorge. It moved with urgency, pulsing and rushing like the blood in her own veins. No matter where she went, even when she had been in Kamloops or Vancouver, she could always hear the roar resonating dully in her ears. She could feel the bridge shudder as the river crashed and swirled around the rocks in its way, slowly, patiently blunting their sharpness.

She had always known the river. She lived on a small bench of land that had been leveled by the river thousands of years before as it ate its way more deeply into the rock. But her feeling for it was more than familiarity: her memory of the river seemed old, ancient. It was a mute memory, an immensely ancient knowledge of the soul of the river.

Though Nancy stood above a single river, just a mile and half east the water split into two rivers. The two were separated by Tschweh, Arrowhead mountain, and they seemed to sneak up on each other, until they rounded the point of the mountain and swirled together, boiling and foaming as they collided.

But they didn't mix, at least not immediately. On one side the clear

1

blue-green water from the north fought off the brown, muddy fingers of the larger river from the east. The whites had their own names for the rivers, but Nancy knew them by the names of her grandmother. The northern river was Kwalatkwa, green river, and the broader river was known as the Kwatequetik, the river that isn't clear. And this place, too, had its own name. Not Creighton, as the townspeople called it, but Hpetkwa, where the waters meet.

Nancy turned her head and looked westward, watching as the two rivers continued their struggle in the canyon below. Gradually the murky waters of the Kwatequetik absorbed the Kwalatkwa until, at the bend about five miles downstream, the river disappeared from sight into a wall of craggy peaks and there was only a thin emerald line against the north shore. Just like our people, the Shuswaps, she thought, reduced to a sliver of what they had once been. And she began to rock again, a tiny figure suspended high above the river, swaying like a leaf in the wind.

Above the low thunder of the river a horn honked impatiently. She looked up to see George's battered pickup parked on the road above the tracks on the south side of the bridge. Even from the middle of the trestle she could see the irregular circles of brown paint surrounding holes rusted through the fenders and doors. The brown splotches against what was left of the green paint gave the truck the look of a well-used World War II surplus vehicle complete with camouflage. As she watched, George waved and shouted something that was drowned out in the roar of the water. She raised her hand in acknowledgement and started toward the truck.

Nancy barely glanced at the ties as she walked slowly across the trestle. Her feet were sure —she had walked the treacherous bridge with its terrifying gaps between the ties many times before. Vaguely she hoped a train wouldn't come. She thought about the times in the past when she had gotten trapped on the bridge. The first time it had happened she was only six. She could remember her father's shout as a train careened out of the trees and thundered onto the bridge. She had quickly lain on the far edge of the ties as her father had ordered, a thousand foot drop on one side, the screaming wheels and shrieking whistle of the train six inches away on the other. A wave of terror swept through her as she remembered the train rushing by her, the trestle jumping and shaking like a wild horse intent on throwing her into the chasm only inches away. She'd pressed her face into the ties, aware only of the sharp smell of the tar, all sound blocked by the screaming of the wheels as they swept by. She'd tried to wrap her legs around the ties to brace against the shaking and had dug her fingers into the ties until she could feel her skin tearing against the hard wood.

Nancy shook her head to try to clear the old memory. That had been the worst time. Later, she had gotten less and less scared, but she still dreaded the sight of the big orange snout with its single eye hurtling toward her. Even now she felt her stomach turn soft as she thought about the bridge shuddering and quivering as the train rolled onto the trestle, its horn blasting a useless warning. With no time to turn back and the sheer drop to the gorge below, there was only the three feet of bare tie for refuge.

As she walked she thought about her aunt who had died on the bridge two years ago. The engineer said she'd just stood on the side as the train approached. "She must have lost her balance," he'd told the police. "Wasn't my fault. What could I do?" And the railway certainly wasn't to blame. After the band had written them about the situation they received a curt reply. "Our hands are tied," they wrote. "We have posted a sign at each end warning people not to go out on the trestle. If they choose to disregard the warning we are not responsible for the consequences." The band's suggestion that a simple walkway and handrail be installed was flatly rejected. "The expenses would run to several thousand dollars," the letter read, "and we are under no obligation whatsoever to provide such a facility." After all, she thought angrily, only Indians live over there anyway.

So no one was responsible and no one was at fault. And yet seven people had died on the bridge over the last few years because the only other way across the river was by a ramshackle ferry that ran three miles upstream and closed at eight in the evening. Nancy felt her bitterness turning into something else, something duller, as she walked the last few feet to the south side of the canyon. It was anger and rage mixed with helplessness, bewilderment, and shame, and it filled her up until she almost choked.

Still seething inside, Nancy climbed up the sandy bank toward the waiting truck. Finally she reached the edge of the broad bench that contained the town and stood on the road.

"For God's sake!" George called from the side of the truck. "Are you in some sort of trance, lady? I thought you were going to camp out there! You're going to be late for school and I was supposed to be at the mill, a half hour ago."

Nancy's eyes shifted from the jumble of houses and buildings to George's face, his eyes rolling in exasperation. He was the handsomest man she had ever seen. His deep brown eyes were almost as black as his pupils, giving his clear, chestnut skin an even darker cast. His long black hair was pulled back in the usual pony tail and tied near his head with a strip of red cloth. As always, a smile played around his lips. She didn't think she'd ever seen George without his smile. It seemed to dance around his face like a warm flame, lighting up his eyes with a dark glow.

Even her silence couldn't put a damper on that flame as she climbed into the truck. "Uh, oh," George muttered teasingly, "looks like you're in one of your moods. Don't I even get a kiss? No? Well, I guess making out is out of the question then."

She stared steadily at the floor while he snorted and chuckled. "You're such a wit," she commented acidly. "Why don't you ever clean this thing?" She gestured at the inside of the truck, littered with candy bar wrappers, beer bottles, chocolate milk cartons and at least a dozen Big Mac containers. "Jeez, it looks like you've been out stealing trash from McDonalds!"

"Naw," George replied. "It's just that the McDonald's stuff is plastic so it doesn't break down as quickly. See, most of the stuff I throw in here gets composted and turns into topsoil. That way when this old truck has the big one and its spirit heads for that big junk yard in the sky, I can park it out in front of the house and plant turnips in it."

Nancy carefully lifted a few layers of trash with the toe of her shoe. Sure enough, tiny green shoots were pushing their way through the debris. "I think it's disgusting," she said.

"You're just not into organic gardening, babe. Why, I think I'll try starting individual pumpkin plants in those Big Mac boxes. This thing could become a regular rolling greenhouse!" Obviously delighted with the idea, George grinned broadly.

Nancy looked out the window as the truck ground into gear and pulled off the sandy shoulder. The old pickup shook and rattled, and the eagle feather tied to the rearview mirror shuddered in sympathy. She slid toward the door, trying to avoid the springs that clawed up through gaping tears in the vinyl upholstery. At some point the rips had been half-heartedly covered with grey duct tape, but the tape had been no match for the springs and had been quickly thrust aside.

4

It now spread itself across the seat like fly paper just waiting to latch onto unwary posteriors.

George reached over to turn on the radio. As he fumbled with a bare stem where a knob should have been, his hand hit a stick that wedged the radio into the hole in the dash. The whole works fell onto the floor, trailing wires like entrails. Nancy shook her head as George tried to replace the radio, turn it on, and drive through town simultaneously.

"George Thomas, would you look where you're going?" Nancy shrieked as the truck lurched straight toward Grebs' store window. George looked up, yanked the wheel to the left, and waved cheerfully to a group of tourists who had flattened themselves in terror against the store.

"Did you see them?" George chortled as the truck roared down the street. "Man, they thought some crazy Indian had traded his pony in for a truck and was after their scalps! Maybe I should go back and have another run at them. What do you say? Maybe they'll circle up the Greyhounds!"

"George, sometimes I think you're out of your mind," Nancy said fiercely. "You almost put your truck in Grebs' display window, taking four innocent bystanders with you — not to mention me — and you think it's all a big joke. Are you going to drive me to school or should I get out and walk?"

George smiled merrily. "School? Oh yeah. I knew we were headed somewhere." He jammed his foot down on the accelerator and the old truck, shrieking in dismay, leaped forward like a stung mare. They flew up from the town on the steep road that wound its way to the high school. She could see it now, hanging over the steep canyon like an enormous buzzard perched on the ledge.

Nancy had never been able to figure out exactly why the school had been located two miles out of town and on the main highway. She had been told once that it was to take advantage of the view. But if that had been the concern why had the place been built with virtually no windows? Perhaps it had more to do with being close to The Heights, the white enclave located just above the highway and as far from the reserve as possible.

As they neared the school the fortress effect became more pronounced. The few narrow windows looked more like gun portals, and the unrelieved grey cinderblock construction gave the structure an air of somberness and gloom.

Nancy hated the school. Not in the same dull, aching way she hated the town, but with a bright, active hatred that flared up like a flame every time she got near the place. But no matter how much she detested it she was going to get through it. It was her ticket out.

As the truck came to a stop by the drive leading to the school, Nancy put her hand where the inside door handle should have been, forgetting that it had been gone for years. George laughed and opened his door, holding it open for her and bowing gallantly. She slid over and climbed out. "I've gotta fix that thing one day," he muttered.

Standing beside him she paused, hooked her arm around his solid waist, and raised herself up to kiss him. "George", she said quietly. "When are we going to get out of here? I want to leave this place."

His smile lost some of its warmth and his eyes grew hard. He stood staring at the wedge of open sky between the steep sides of the canyon. From here they could see about six miles up the canyon to the west before the mountains closed ranks. Behind them the two rivers thrust to the north and east, quickly disappearing into the ranges that flanked them. All around them the mountains seemed to form a solid, impenetrable wall.

George pointed west to the point where the river bent out of sight and the peaks seemed to join like clasped fingers. His finger traced the ragged boundaries of the canyon eastward, then continued its jagged elipse around the northern perimeter until he was pointing west again. He lowered his arm. "This is the world." He spoke slowly, barely moving his lips. "It begins there and ends there." He seemed to shake himself and some of the lightness came back into his face. "This is my world," he laughed. "There's nothing else out there. What kind of nonsense are they feeding you in that place anyway?"

She looked at him silently for a moment. "I mean it George. We've got to get out. This town is a killer, and you know it."

"Well, right now I'm more worried about my boss," George smiled, getting back into his truck and slamming the door twice trying to get it to catch. "I *know* he's a killer, and I'm already an hour late for work. See you tonight."

The truck squealed off in a spray of gravel and dust. At the highway, George stopped at the stop sign and opened the door. He stood on the rusty running board and blew her a kiss before wheeling around the turn and heading for the mill. Nancy waved and turned toward the school.

II.

Entering the school was like climbing through the mouth of the old mine shaft out by Marble Lake. Nancy had once entered it on a dare. In the building, sunlight was replaced by gloomy corridors lit by the glare of fluorescent lights, and the warmth of the day was replaced with a metallic coldness. Somewhere down behind mysterious locked doors deep in the basement a giant air conditioner was methodically refrigerating the place. Nancy could almost see frost forming on the walls. She thought she could feel the floors throbbing to the soundless hum of the thing.

She stood inside the door uncertainly. On her left were the yellow doors into the gym and to her right was the hallway with its bright orange doors into the stark cinderblock and vinyl classrooms. In front of her, in the office, Doughnut Stephenson was sitting grimly behind the glass as she pounded on typewriter keys. She was the school secretary, and as long as anyone could remember she'd worn her greying hair pulled back in the thick bun that gave her the nickname. Nancy could try to sneak by her and get into the classroom without being seen, but she had biology first period — Quigley — and that was bad news. He would be sure to mark her late, and then she would be called down to the office to face charges of being late *and* neglecting to sign in. It was better to face Doughnut's wrath now than on a double rap later.

Nancy walked through the door into the office and up to the counter. Doughnut refused to acknowledge her and continued attacking the typewriter as though it had offended her in some way. Nancy slapped her books down loudly.

"I am aware of your presence, Miss Antoine," Doughnut snapped in her clipped English accent. "There is no need to bang about."

Nancy bit back a reply and stood mutely. Finally Doughnut ripped the paper out of the typewriter and slammed it down on the table. She stood up and eyed Nancy with distaste.

"Late again, Miss Antoine? The sixth time this month. What's your excuse today?"

Something flared in Nancy, and she heard herself say, "Oh, well I had a breakfast meeting with the prime minister."

Doughnut's eyes grew wide then narrowed dangerously. A red rash crept up her neck. "Don't you get impertinent with me," she

7

hissed, "I can have you out of here so fast it'll take your breath away."

Nancy knew she wasn't kidding. It was Doughnut who ran the school, not Mr. Patterson the principal. He cowered behind his closed doors most of the day, emerging only to hand a letter to Doughnut or pick up a memo. He viewed the world through his secretary's eyes. If she wanted Nancy out, all Doughnut needed to do was feed him some acid comments about Nancy's attendance and behaviour and she was a goner.

Nancy lowered her eyes and mumbled an apology. "Uh, sorry Miss Stephenson. It's been a hard week."

Doughnut nodded slightly. "That's better. Now sign in. Any more unexcused absences this month will be reported to Mr. Patterson."

Nancy quickly signed the sheet in the black binder and picked up her books. As she walked down the hall she fought back the angry tears that welled in her eyes. Finding herself in front of her classroom she hesitated before opening the door, and steeled herself for Quigley's remarks.

Quigley was probably the most hated person at Creighton Secondary. It wasn't just that he ran the dullest classroom in the school or even that he was nasty to the point of being cruel. There was something even more insidious about the man. Whatever she could say about the other teachers in the school, Nancy at least felt that in their own way they wanted their students to learn, to succeed. They might not have the vaguest idea of how to relate to students, and their lectures might have all the zip and freshness of flat beer, but at least they hoped their students would do well. But Quigley was different. He seemed to delight in failing students, especially Indian students. He bullied and intimidated, harrying Indian pupils into withdrawal as if he needed to constantly prove his own dark bigotries through their failure.

Like last week when he had confronted Amanda Johnny in class. He had collected papers that were due that day and Amanda's wasn't there. He stalked down the aisle and stood over her like some livid demon. "Where is your paper, young lady? Have you ever gotten a paper in on time?" Amanda sat quietly and stared at her desk, which seemed to enrage Quigley even more. "Answer me when I ask a question," he screamed, pounding on the desk with his fist. "And look at me when I'm speaking to you!" Amanda sat as rigid as stone and Quigley flew into an absolute rage. His usually ruddy face flushed a bright crimson, the veins in his broad forehead standing out like thick strings. "I will not tolerate disrespect and insolence in my classroom," he raged, thrusting his face inches from hers. "If you do not look at me and answer me this instant I will have you suspended from school!"

Nancy had felt her stomach tighten until it hurt. She looked around the room, but everyone's eyes were averted. Amanda suffered, totally alone, humiliated and powerless. But just as horrible was the inaction of the class. And of Nancy. She desperately wanted to stop the ordeal, but she too sat watching in agony, silent.

Finally even Quigley had had enough. Amanda had never shown the slightest response. He stood up and pointed at the door. "Get out!" he snarled. "Now!"

Amanda had quickly picked up her books and slunk quietly through the door. Quigley had gotten her suspended for two days. But Amanda would never be back.

One thought kept pounding in Nancy's head: we were all too scared to lift a finger to stop the pain.

Now she opened the door as quietly as possible and slipped toward her seat. Quigley had his back to her as he scribbled the parts of a fish on a diagram drawn on the board. Each student had an identical diagram on a sheet of paper and was dutifully copying down the parts —anterior, posterior, lateral, ventral—as Quigley wrote them on the board. She glanced down at Tom Charlie's paper and noticed that he had drawn a bra on his fish and had a balloon coming out of its mouth. "When the going gets tough," he had written, "the tough go fishing!" Nancy tried to stifle a giggle, but it was too late. She'd been noticed.

Quigley whirled around from the board and placed his hands on the back of his chair. He leaned forward, thrusting his big raw face toward her. Even across the room she could see the network of veins in his ruddy cheeks and the bushy eyebrows that hung like partially drawn curtains over the tiny deepset eyes. He jabbed the chalk at her.

"I see that it's not enough," he sputtered, "to insult me and the rest of the class by arriving late. But now that you have condescended to attend you insist on disturbing the other students with your inane giggling. Sit down, Miss Antoine, and I'll see you after school."

Like hell you will, thought Nancy as she slid into her seat and opened her biology book. There was yet another diagram of a fish, all parts colour coded. Geez, she thought, when it comes to things

9

that are really important, like the parts of a fish, you just can't repeat them too much.

The period crawled by with agonizing slowness. Nancy felt her head pitch forward as she dozed off. She caught herself before slamming into the hard formica desk top, but almost immediately her eyes began to droop again. She tried desperately to find some kind of diversion, but it was impossible to make contact with other students. They either gazed numbly into space or stared with unfocussed eyes at their books. She tried to study the mountains through the narrow window slots at each end of the room, but all she could see was the bank of raw dirt outside that one day might be landscaped. My God, she thought, it's only 9:15.

Nancy practically sprinted for the hall when the period had mercifully dragged to an end. Leaning up against the lockers she squeezed her eyes shut. How much longer could she stand this? She sensed someone standing in front of her and opened her eyes a crack. Even between her lashes she recognized the unmistakable bulk and shock of blonde hair. Mark Bateman, basketball star, class valedictorian, and general creep was trying to hit on her again.

"What's the trouble, Baby?" Mark said, clenching and unclenching his fists and slowly rotating his massive shoulders as though he was on a dance floor. "Old Quigley give you a rough time?"

"Mark, I don't know who's a bigger geek, you or Quigley."

Mark feigned a hurt expression. "Now is that any way to talk to a guy you're going out with this Saturday?"

"Mark, how can I make it clear? I not only don't want to go out with you, it disturbs me that we have to share the same planet. One of the best reasons to leave this town, and there are lots of good ones, is to avoid your arrogant, bumbling attempts at charm."

Nancy turned and started down the hall. "You just don't know what you're missing," he called after her.

"I can hardly stand the suspense," muttered Nancy.

She almost fled down the stairs to her home economics class. Thank God for Bernice Wu, Nancy thought, as she walked into the class early. Bernice's class — Bernice insisted everyone call her by her first name — was like an oasis. Nancy couldn't quite put her finger on why. It wasn't just that she was nice — most of the teachers were nice outside of class, even though what they taught was useless — or that she was relaxed, though she certainly was. It was something more. She really cared about the people in her class, not just as students but as people. She was the only teacher who asked about the students' families, or even seemed to know they had families. Once Nancy's father had gotten drunk and fell down an icy embankment, breaking a leg. Nancy had been called in the middle of the night and walked across the bridge to the hospital. The next day Bernice, gentle concern in her brown eyes, had asked how he was. Then, seeing the fatigue in Nancy's face, she had put her arm around the girl's shoulders. "Listen, you go and get some sleep," she suggested. "I'll tell the office I sent you home because you were ill."

And Bernice was always there, in school or out, to talk. Her classroom and home were always open. But something else made her special too. Maybe it was the way she worked with students, gliding quietly around the room, helping, waiting patiently, helping again. And she never seemed to need to be asked for assistance. Somehow she just knew and was there. There didn't seem to be the physical barrier there was with other teachers either. Sometimes it was as simple as brushing shoulders, but occasionally she would, just out of sheer joy and affection, hug someone. It was a little shocking at first, but as students realized the genuineness of her gestures, they came to appreciate and then love the woman who glowed like a warm ember in the ashes of a dead fire.

As Nancy put her books on a counter and sat on a stool, she looked up to see Bernice's smiling face. Maybe it was just her smile, thought Nancy. Maybe it's as simple as that. It was as warm and genuine as Bernice herself. Today it was especially appreciated.

"How's it going?" Bernice asked.

Nancy shrugged. "So far I've been threatened by Doughnut and humiliated by Quigley. And it's just second period."

"Say, sounds like just another average day at Creighton Secondary," Bernice grinned. "I'll get the medic. We've been known to give aid and comfort to the enemy in here. And look on the bright side: graduation is just three months away."

Other students were beginning to straggle into class. Most were female, but a few males were courageous enough to take a course that taught the most practical skills offered while having to endure the insults and taunts of the Mark Batemans of the school. Jacob Worabey settled in next to her.

"I heard the Mad Bull of the science department gored you pretty good today."

Nancy shrugged and smiled. Jacob was one of the few white students who seemed to try to relate to her as a full-fledged member of the human race. "Yeah. His gore is worse than his bite. I've been subjected to both."

Nancy worked through the period with Rose Jack and Jacob. The class was preparing food for a lunch to be held the next day for a group of elders from the reserve. It was practically the only time they ever penetrated the walls of the school. Her group was working on baking bread, but they would also be frying bannock before the dinner. Nancy liked working in groups. While they worked they talked easily and laughed. Rose was talking about her three-year-old sister. "She loves telling jokes," Rose giggled, "but they never make sense. Like yesterday she asked, 'Why did the chicken cross the road? Because the boy wore green pants.'"

"Sounds to me like she's getting into Zen Buddhism," Jacob commented.

The respite soon ended. She contemplated what was ahead of her: social studies before lunch with its endless story of Canadian Confederation. Two periods of English after lunch, full of prepositional phrases, faulty parallelism and literature as far removed from her reality as possible. Then algebra, hours of sitting alone, mired in skeins of strange, useless numbers and letters. She passed by the locked glass case where the awards were kept. There were a few minor sports trophies, a list of graduates arranged by year, and a plaque with the names of the recipients of last term's academic awards. Nine out of ten were white, Nancy thought, in a school that is more than half Indian. And the one Indian guy who snuck in was about as Indian as Stanley Quigley. He lived in a white foster home and regarded the Indian students with the sort of disdain and disgust that only a convert can feel.

But Nancy was going to get her name up there on this year's graduate list. She told herself she could put up with three more months of boredom. When Indian students looked around they saw failure for themselves and success for the handful of white students. It was the Indian students who were slotted into the vocational tracks. It was the Indian students who ended up in remedial classes. It was they who found themselves at the bottom of the class standings. But who could blame the school? After all, it had the weight of the cinder block building and the expertise of college-trained educators. Teachers knew their subjects, and administrators sternly indicated that success was equally available to all. Who could argue with the school? So there had to be something wrong with them, the students. The Indians.

Nancy knew there was more to it than that. This was the explanation the schools wanted them to accept, but Nancy remembered things too clearly. She recalled her wide-eyed panic as she was shoved into a grade one classroom with a white teacher who jumped up and down, flailing her arms, her voice rising and falling like she was berserk. Nancy remembered, too, a bunch of white students who acted exactly the same way as she sat silently, trying to figure out what those people were doing, feeling more and more alone as the Indian kids slid deeper into their little desks, afraid even to look at each other.

It wasn't long before she noticed that when she and other Indian kids held the unfamiliar books full of unfamiliar faces and words, they found themselves in the reading groups where boys and girls read haltingly or not at all. Then the teacher began to frown at them. And when she had been singled out and told to read in front of the class she'd wanted to sink through the floor. When Nancy thought about that even now, eleven years later, she shuddered in remembered shame and terror. She'd sat there dumb and frightened, unaccustomed to performing on command or in front of a group.

Soon she came to hate and fear the classroom with its daily terror, loneliness, and humiliation. Where were the words and soft smiles of her home and relatives? Where was the gentle encouragement of her grandmother and the wonderful trips up into the valleys to pick berries and play in the sunflowers?

The results of all this loss, all this hurt, were too clear. By grade three most of her friends saw themselves as failures, and by grade eight they had failed one or two grades. But somehow Nancy hung on, and soon she became stronger and more bitter, but determined. She couldn't fully understand or explain what was wrong with the school — it was too vague and confusing, and thinking about it just made her angry and frustrated — but she could be one who made it, who waded through all the crap and got out alive. And she would do it as an Indian.

A group of younger Indian boys pushed past her, uniformed in cut-off jean jackets with the names of various rock bands stitched crudely on the back. They were oblivious to her or anyone else. She saw that one of them was her first cousin Pat Antoine. He was pretending to drive.

"Man, when I get some money together I'm gonna buy the biggest four-by-four you've ever seen. I'm gonna roar up the logging roads like a mad man, spewing gravel all over the place. Maybe I'll even enter that mud bog race over in Falkland. That'd be great!" Pat made sounds of a straining motor.

Nancy shook her head. She didn't know whether to be disgusted or depressed. "Damn it, Pat, when are you going to grow up?" she snapped.

Pat just sneered at her and kept on shifting gears down the hallway.

Suddenly the bell screamed above her head. She flinched instinctively and darted toward her social studies class. Zachary Taylor, their young teacher, paced nervously in front of the class. He always seemed somewhat frantic. His lectures — and that's what most of the classes consisted of — were essentially summaries of the reading assignments, adding little or nothing to the subjects. But Taylor seemed to try to make up for the failure of his material with what he probably saw as enthusiasm. He gestured dramatically, lashing the air as he spoke. All this activity and angularity just made Nancy nervous. She had a vague fear that one of his boney elbows was going to slam into her temple during one of his more energetic gestures.

Today Taylor launched into a vigorous review, almost word for word from the text, of the Canadian Confederation debates.

"These were men of great wisdom. Cartier, MacDonald, and Brown were all men of fierce convictions. But they were willing to put philosophical differences aside to create a new nation. They knew that the only thing between them and a country from the Atlantic to the Pacific was regional mistrust and a lack of imagination."

"Yeah, and a few hundred thousand Indians," muttered Cyril Narcisse from the back.

Taylor faltered for a moment. "Well, yes, that too. But, ahem, that's another issue. We won't get into that this year." He quickly regained his stride. "Where today is the boldness, the courage, the vision these men had? Where is the willingness to face the issues squarely and resolutely?"

Nancy could feel her face flush. She hated talking out in class, but

14

suddenly she felt she had to. "How about the bridge? Let's talk about an issue that affects us here. Our people here and now. Why don't we talk about that? It's more important than talking about what a bunch of guys did a hundred years ago. Why don't we talk about that?" Nancy had to stop and breath deeply. Taylor had stopped in mid-gesture, his arm still raised in the air.

Nancy spoke more calmly now, but more intensely. "You're always talking about what changes people made in their lives in the past. Why not help us learn to make changes for our people's lives now? Seven people have died on that bridge. We have to force the railroad to put up a walkway. Help us organize. We could get up a petition or stage a blockade." At this Taylor began to motion his open hand toward her as if to soothe her. "Help us *do* something," she finished.

Taylor gulped once. Then he took a step back and sat on his desk. He shook his head. "Nancy," he began in his most patient, forbearing voice. "Those are interesting ideas, but we just don't have the time. We will be hard pressed to finish the text as it is. Furthermore, that sort of, uh, topic is not in the curriculum. You should take this matter up with your band." Having regained his composure and the initiative, Taylor resumed. "As I was saying, on March 11, 1865, at four in the morning, the question of Confederation came to a vote by the members from Canada East and West. The vote was ninety-one to thirty-three in favour and..."

Nancy went limp. Her outburst had hardly caused a ripple. The class was back on track, hurtling ahead into a tunnel of lifeless facts and meaningless details.

Taylor's words droned on. Through the narrow windows at the front she could just get a glimpse of the river struggling through the rugged walls of the canyon. She was tired, tired of struggling. Three more hours. Not today.

At the bell she walked out of school into the bright spring sunshine and headed down the hill. She wouldn't be back that afternoon. They had won, she thought, this day.

III.

The spring sunshine warmed Nancy's back as she walked down the road that twisted from the school to the town below. Snow still covered the upper half of the mountains. Below that, the ponderosa pines dotted the lower slopes distinctly and separately, like those in a child's drawing, standing out in relief against the dry, rocky background. These slopes flattened out in benches, patches of green that hovered above the river, their sharp edges plummeting into the swirling water.

The benches were the only land suitable for farming. Nancy thought bitterly how, long ago, the biggest and best farmland had been given to white farmers, leaving the band with dozens of tiny fields, rarely more than a few acres, that were of little agricultural value. Years before, she'd been told, Indians used to grow beans on their tiny plots and shipped them to distant markets. But as the market shrank and the cost of production increased, the small plots became uneconomical. Only the large ranches that had enough capital to diversify into cattle and fruit, install irrigation, and mechanize remained viable. And because the Indians were not trained in agriculture — except for the four hours a day of backbreaking field work the boys had to perform in residential schools — the small plots slipped out of production one by one and the Indians slipped further into poverty and dependence.

Nancy remembered standing in Grebs' store with her father. She couldn't have been more than six or seven. While slowly checking their purchases, Simon Grebs was chatting with the local hotel and pub owner, Larry Mills, a fat, violent man who scared Nancy. She had seen him throw Indians out of the pub, kicking them as they lay helpless on the ground until his fury was exhausted. This morning he was loafing in Grebs' store, leaning against the sacks of rice.

"Damn lazy Indians," he growled. "They get all this land and do nothing with it. Why, they used to produce all kinds of beans. Now they don't grow nothin' but kids." He gave a short, harsh laugh.

She and her father stood there, Nancy clutching his leg and looking out fearfully at this big, loud man, while her father stared at the cartons and cans on the counter. It was as though she and he weren't there, as though they were invisible.

Grebs nodded his head. "I know, I know, but what can you do?

They get so much on welfare they don't need to work."

Her father was still working at the mill then, but he said nothing. He just pulled out his old leather wallet and counted out the money for the bill.

"Give that land to a white man and see what could be done, eh?" Mills went on.

Her father picked up the bags of groceries and carried them out to the old truck. Before they were out the door Grebs had turned to Mills. "Did you hear the one about how to catch an Indian? No? Well..."

Mercifully, the door closed. Nancy was young, but her stomach seethed as she climbed into the cab of the old pickup. How could her father say nothing? Would those men have hurt him if he had? Were those white men right? Tears of humiliation and helplessness streamed down her cheeks.

Her father climbed silently into the truck. It shuddered to life as he turned the key. They drove in silence for several minutes. Then he spoke to her.

"Those men are hateful men," he said slowly. "They have no love and no heart. They are like vultures. They came here to live off the Indians and we Indians keep them here. They don't even wait for us to die. They eat us alive." He paused. "They eat us and grow fat. If it was not for us they would starve, they would die. And they know it and they hate us for it. But somehow they have gained the power." He gave a short laugh. "My grandfather insisted they prayed to death spirits, that they used bad medicine. I don't know, but we don't know how to fight them. Maybe you will learn how."

Nancy remembered that dark day as though it had been only hours before. But this day was bright, and she was alone among the sunflowers that sprang from the thin soil. The yellow blossoms were held by sturdy short stems and framed by the thick leaves. They studded the hillsides like yellow jewels. Her grandmother had shown her how to dig the thick taproots and roast them. Not many people did that now, nor did many go up into the high valley and dig wild potatoes or lily roots. She could remember spring days like this one when her family had gone up in the old green truck, her grandmother, father and mother in the cab, she sitting on a pile of sacks in the back.

There were always other families digging too, and the outing became a picnic. Kettles were boiled for tea and the fresh potatoes, sometimes cooked with Indian celery, were boiled in pots. They were tender and sweet.

All that had seemed to stop when her mother had left. Oh, her aunts and uncles would still take her places, but it wasn't the same. Somehow the joy had gone. Her father withdrew more and more, leaving her alone, and slowly the outings stopped. She wondered how many people still went up to the valley in the spring.

Nancy stopped by one of the sunflowers and felt the fuzzy centre. Suddenly a horn blasted just inches behind her. It wasn't the normal honk of a car horn but the full-throated roar of a semi bearing down on her. Nancy jumped forward, landing face down on the gravel. Her heart pounding, she rolled over and stared up fearfully. Instead of a massive truck crashing by inches away, she saw the faded red of a tiny rust-spotted Datsun stopped on the road. Inside she could see Barry Paul pounding on the dashboard in hysterics.

Nancy leaped to her feet and rushed over to the car, kicking the door furiously. "You jerk!" she shrieked. "You almost scared me to death!"

Through the open window, Nancy started lashing at Barry, who was too weak from laughing to defend himself. Finally he managed to wind up the window. Nancy continued beating on the glass. Then she bent over and picked up a large rock.

"If you don't come out of there," Nancy screamed, "I'm going to smash that window in and come after you. You just try me and see if I don't do it!"

Barry held his hands up, palms flat against the glass in surrender. "OK," he yelled. "I give up. Just promise you won't hit me if I get out!"

"I'm not promising anything! Get out of there and take your chances, you wimp."

Barry climbed slowly out of the car. He was trying to suppress his laughter, but the effort was too much. Guffaws and snickers erupted as he held out his hands defensively toward Nancy.

Nancy sized him up. He was a little guy but wiry. She thought she could at least knock him onto the ground once. She raised the rock menacingly and advanced toward him.

"Listen," Barry pleaded between snickers. "I'm sorry. Really, I am. I just installed that air horn and I didn't even know how loud it would be. Come on, truce, OK?"

She looked at his dark face with its shiny teeth and its sharp features. "Boy, Barry," she snarled. "If I didn't like you, you'd be eating broken teeth for lunch." Nancy dropped the rock on the roadside.

Barry came over and gave her a hug. "Listen, I am sorry, but you sure looked funny sprawled out there like someone had kicked you in the rear. I meant to surprise you, not stampede you."

Nancy managed a little smile. "I guess it was pretty funny. But damn it, Barry," she said more fiercely, "don't sneak up on people that way."

"I didn't sneak up on you. I saw you on the side of the road and came over to see if you wanted a ride. Man, you were somewhere else. I just honked the old horn here" — Barry reached into the car and grabbed a handle hanging underneath the dash. An enormous blast shook the little car — "to get your attention. Neat eh? I pulled it out of a wrecked truck."

Nancy had calmed down and decided that what he was saying was probably true. Besides he was George's best friend. "OK, all is forgiven. Give me a ride downtown and we'll forget about it."

Nancy opened the passenger door and surveyed the interior with disgust. Dr. Pepper cans, spark plugs, old oil filters, wads of paper and empty oil containers covered the floor. "Yuck! Do you and George buy your garbage from the same dump?"

"How insulting." Barry climbed in through the driver's door. "I maintain a much better class of garbage. If you're brave enough to plow through George's junk all you find is more junk. But if you drill through mine you hit oil." Nancy delicately moved some of the debris aside. Sure enough, underneath was at least a half inch of caked grease and dirty oil.

"This is absolutely nauseating, Barry. Why can't you guys clean your vehicles?" Nancy carefully placed two Dr. Pepper cans on the floor and rested her shoes on them.

She glanced in the back. A candy bar box full of crude arrow heads was sitting on the seat. Nancy groaned.

"Barry, you're not selling arrowheads again, are you?"

Barry looked at her brightly. "Of course. It's almost tourist season."

"Barry, you know you're ripping people off by making those things in your house and passing them off as genuine."

"But they *are* genuine. Genuine arrowheads. What's more,

they're made by a genuine Indian. Me. I mean I'm just an entrepreneurial sort of guy, a small businessman. Isn't that what makes this country great? I can't help it if demand exceeds supply. I mean it's a dirty job but someone's got to do it."

"You know one day you're going to get busted for this," Nancy said darkly, her brown eyes reproachful.

"For what? What are the charges? Selling deadly weapons without a license? Manufacturing armaments for illegal export? Maybe quarrying shale without provincial permission. Listen, I'm just following a time-honoured European tradition — I'm selling useless trinkets to local inhabitants for a hundred times their actual value. Hey, we should know all about that."

Nancy shook her head. "You know perfectly well what I mean. You're selling these things under false pretenses. You lead people to believe these are old, and that's not right."

Barry shrugged his shoulders and winked. "Let the buyer beware. Anyway, I'll bet these rocks are millions of years old. Listen, I'm thinking about taking a business management course so I can expand. Maybe I can get a government business loan. Who knows? Maybe this will prove the economic salvation of Creighton."

By this time they had wound down the hill and were entering the town. Creighton was strung along a narrow bench that dropped abruptly several hundred feet to the river. The railroad ran along the rim and paralleled the main road that ran through town. Nancy looked out at the bleak little row of houses and shops. Several stores were boarded and the only gas station downtown, where Barry had worked as a mechanic, had closed the year before. The liquor store, with its barred windows, remained as busy as ever, and further down the street the Creighton pub, a squat white stucco building that thrust its double doors onto the sidewalk, also thrived. The pub was attached to the old two-storey hotel, which, with its long porch and second-storey balconies, looked like part of the set of a western movie.

Across the street was the new RCMP station. The sheriff's office, Nancy thought. And beyond that was the invisible boundary between Creighton and the reserve. The Indians lived on one side in deteriorating Department of Indian Affairs plywood shacks; the whites were on the other in a handful of older houses and lines of rusting mobile homes. The town was as segregated as any community in South Africa, right down to the churches and cemeteries. Two Catholic churches, one for the four hundred whites in town, one for the twelve hundred Indians, stood a half mile apart. And separate cemeteries insured that the colour line would remain intact even after death.

God, what a place! thought Nancy. What was she doing here? How many more days before she could get out, forever?

Barry nudged her. "Hey, where are you today? I just asked you where you want to get off."

Nancy looked away from the sad collection of buildings and stared across the river. The mountain peaks glowed like massive lighthouses. The light appeared too bright to be just reflection; it seemed to be emanating from some enormous internal power source surging through the mountain crests.

Barry had stopped the car and was shaking her shoulder. "Nancy are you all right?" He looked at her with concern.

Nancy shook herself and quickly glanced at him. "Sorry. Sorry, Barry. I was just, you know, thinking."

Barry was silent for a moment. "Yeah. I think I do know." For several seconds there was quiet in the car, the silence stirred only by the noise of the clock, which, though three hours and twenty minutes slow, miraculously kept working.

Finally Barry repeated his question softly. "Where do you want to get off, Nancy?"

"Grebs' I guess," Nancy said. "I have to pick up some groceries for my Dad and me. He doesn't have anything for dinner."

"Are you sure he's at home? I mean..." Barry's voice trailed off into a mumble.

"You mean is he in the pub?" Nancy shrugged. "I don't think so. He was so sick this morning that he wouldn't try to get across there. Besides, he promised me he wouldn't. But he hasn't had anything decent to eat in two days." Nancy looked at the books on the seat. "Barry, would you give me a ride down to the ferry? George was going to give me a lift, but I, uh, I got done a little early."

Barry grinned. "Right. I got done a little early almost every day I went to school. Sure I'll give you a ride. The arrowhead business has been a little slow anyway."

"Do you want to come in?"

Barry's face darkened. "I only go into Grebs' when starvation forces me into his claws. No thanks, I'll wait out here."

Nancy ran across the street and into the small grocery store. She hated shopping there. It wasn't just the distrustful, arrogant glare of Grebs that she hated or the pain of old memories; it was also the exorbitant prices. She fingered a small package of hamburger, knowing it was at least twice as much as she would pay in a larger centre. But in Creighton it was Grebs' prices or nothing. Most of the whites and many of the Indians drove to Kamloops for supplies, but the poorest had no vehicles or couldn't afford the cost of gas. Others were dependent on the credit that Grebs extended while charging high rates of interest.

Gritting her teeth, Nancy filled a small basket and walked to the front of the store. Simon Grebs, shrunken like an Egyptian mummy, stood at the cash register, his bony fingers playing lovingly over the keys. He peered over his bifocals at Rita Thomas, who was waiting at the counter. Nancy smiled at Roger and Lily, two of Rita's children. Slowly, Rita pushed a cheque over to Grebs, who picked it up and scanned it briefly. Then he placed it in his open cash drawer and took out a couple of twenties.

Rita stood fingering the two bills quietly, puzzled. Finally she said softly, "Mr. Grebs, that cheque was for $240. My groceries only came to $65. I should get $175, but you only gave me $40."

Grebs briskly shut the drawer and started drawing Nancy's items toward the register. "You owe me $200, Rita. I'm taking the rest of that cheque as payment."

Rita's voice never rose, but her tone became desperate, pleading. "Please, Mr. Grebs. That's all I have for the month. I've got bills to pay. Forty dollars isn't enough."

Grebs never looked at her. "That's too bad, Rita. Maybe next time you'll keep your bill paid. This is a business, not a charity."

Rita gathered up her bags and walked quietly out the door. Lily held onto Rita's skirts and looked back with frightened eyes.

Nancy stood frozen. Grebs added up her items and checked the register. "That's $24.85."

Still Nancy stood motionless.

"What's the problem with you?" Grebs rasped. "Are you going to pay or do I have to put all this back?"

Nancy looked up. Grebs' gaunt face was thrust toward her. "Mr. Grebs," Nancy whispered, her voice shaking, "that wasn't right. You can't just take people's money like that. She has nothing..."

"Listen you," Grebs snarled, "you'd better mind your own business or I'll bar you from the store. Don't start moralizing to me, you little breed brat, or you and that drunken old man of yours will never set foot in here again." He straightened up and gave a harsh laugh. "If you don't like the way I do business try the competition."

Nancy's heart was pounding as if it would explode. Choking back anger and fear, she fished a twenty and a five from her pocket. She grabbed her small bag of groceries and fled from the store.

"Hey, don't you want your change?" Grebs sneered behind her.

Nancy didn't look back. She plunged blindly through the door, onto the sidewalk, and into the street. A car slammed on its brakes to avoid her. She didn't hear the curses hurled at her by the driver as she ran for Barry's car. She reached the door and collapsed to her knees, sobbing. Barry helped her in and then sat quietly as she tried to catch her breath. She told him what happened.

Suddenly he began pounding the steering wheel rhythmically with mounting fury. "God damn it, God damn it!" he raged as his palm smashed the hard plastic of the wheel. "How long do we have to take this?" Suddenly he reached for the door handle. "I'll kill him," he whispered.

"No," Nancy cried. "Let's just go! Please."

Barry slowly closed the door and put the car in gear. They drove in silence.

"Barry, Grebs isn't the only problem anymore," Nancy said, now calm and thoughtful. "We've been made to accept our situation. Why can't we stop a monster like that from humiliating another generation of our people, from charging outrageous prices, from hooking our poorest people into high interest rates? Why can't we start our own store? Form a food co-op? Other bands are doing it."

"I thought you were leaving," Barry said in a curiously flat, emotionless voice. "Isn't that your solution?"

"I am, but you're not," she burst out at him almost angrily. "You're bright and creative, and what do you do? Chip out arrowheads and fool around with truck horns and old car parts. Why don't you do something? Get the training we need to run a co-op. Help your community, your people. Do something!"

They drove for a long time in silence, passing through the town and down the sandy road that led to the vehicle ramp and the ferry, which was really little more than a floating platform attached to cables strung across the river. She could see Maurice Joe putting blocks under Pete Walkem's pickup.

"Listen, Barry," Nancy said softly. "I'm sorry. It just gets so

24

frustrating. And then we blow up at each other. I'm sorry."

"I know," Barry said. "It's OK."

"Listen, I'm coming back over tonight. I told George that if I missed him this afternoon I would meet him at the pub at eight. Do you want to come?"

Barry thought for a moment then smiled. "Sure," he said. "I'll see you there. You'd better hurry, though." He nodded at the ferry. "They're ready to leave."

Nancy grabbed her groceries and books and hurried toward the make-shift ferry. As she climbed over the rough loading ramp and onto the thick planks of the ferry, she felt the restlessness and power of the river beneath her.

IV.

The road from the ferry to Nancy's home was not more than a half mile, but each step seemed to take her farther into another time, another place. The town was shelved on the opposite bank of the river. Over here there was just the sandy road winding through ponderosa pines and scattered houses, most of them linked to the road by rutted drives that led down to small benches. The smell of pine and awakening earth filled the air. Dry brown needles paved the road, cushioning her footsteps so that she walked almost silently.

Over here the pace was slower, so slow that some families still relied on horse-drawn wagons for transportation. On Saturdays Nancy would see whole families in wagons, parents and older children on the seat, younger kids and grandparents jouncing in the back as the wagons creaked slowly toward the ferry on a trip into town to get supplies. They came from Six Mile, Twelve Mile and Twenty-Two Mile, all family compounds huddled above the river where people still lived much as they had for a hundred years.

Even the people near the ferry were different. The river was only a few hundred feet wide, but it separated two countries, two realities. Shuswap was often spoken here, even by the young people. Though most had been to residential school they had returned to families and values that remained intact and solid.

There wasn't total isolation, of course. She smiled as she passed a tiny dome made of scrap lumber and used windows, an ashram for an Eastern religious group — was it Hindu or Buddhist? — based in Vancouver. There were usually a few men and women there meditating and just "getting in tune with the rhythms of the land". But that was OK. The land was strong enough to heal more than just her people, and at least these came with respect and gentleness. What she dreaded most were the loggers rumored to be headed up the canyon. Why can't they leave us alone? she wondered. They've taken everything else; why can't they leave us this?

The road rose sharply, then dropped into a hollow. A tiny stream rushed down the mountains on her right and tumbled over stones as it hurried toward the river. A simple plank bridge crossed the stream. This was one of Nancy's favourite spots in the world. She stopped on the bridge. The late afternoon sun filtered through the pine needles and emerging willow leaves. Moss grew along the banks of the

27

stream. Rocks above the road walled the hollow in on one side, and dense brush closed in downhill. Nancy was in the centre of a tiny pocket of green and calm. The water in the swollen spring stream rattled beneath the bridge. She breathed deeply the cold, damp air and felt safe.

As far back as she could remember she had paused here on her way home. It was also where she came when she was scared and hurt. In those terrible days after her mother left she had spent hours dangling her feet over the bridge and listening to the stream and the leaves rustling in the wind. Here she was invisible, protected.

Now she crossed the bridge and followed the road around the shoulder of granite that closed off the far side of the hollow. The road rose slightly for a hundred yards, then bent right, but Nancy followed a rough track that turned left and meandered through the trees toward the river. She walked for a few minutes down the gently sloping sandy rut until she reached a clearing. On her left, two dilapidated old trucks sank into the weeds. On her right, in only slightly better shape, was her father's pickup. Rust had eaten around the doors and wheel wells to mock the great swatches of orange rust paint which almost obliterated the original colour.

Beside it was their house, a small structure covered with weathered cedar shakes. It had been built in the 1930's by her grandfather, and over the years, as the family had grown, new rooms had been added until the original one-room log house had expanded into a long, rambling, decaying collection of five rooms, two porches, numerous entrances and three chimneys. She walked across the front porch, carefully avoiding the rotten boards, and opened the front door. In the kitchen, once the entire house, a string of windows ran along the right-hand wall and in the far corner there was an old white enamelled wood stove. The table, covered with red and white checked oil cloth, sat in the middle of the floor.

Nancy put the groceries on the counter and went looking for her father. She crossed the sloping floor to the living room, originally added as a bedroom and, not seeing him resting as he liked to on the old stuffed couch by the fireplace, she went toward the bedrooms, blankets hanging across their doorways. A peek through the right-hand doorway into her father's room revealed that the bed was empty, and a quick glance in her room confirmed that he wasn't there either. She threw her books on the bed.

Another doorway led to the room that had been added when her father was a boy. He and his two brothers had once slept there, and another fireplace had been built to heat the addition. Now the room was used as a pantry and as her father's shop. A table against one wall was covered with half-carved cedar totem poles and plaques. Shavings littered the bare wood floor. His carving tools were hung on a rack that was nailed to the wall.

A final door stood ajar. Nancy pushed through it to the back porch. Her father was sitting in an ancient green easy chair, the once-patterned upholstery worn slick with time. His head was stretched back so that his eyes, if they'd been open, would have been staring directly at the boards of the ceiling. She heard him snoring softly.

When Nancy saw him like this, sprawled out, his feet stretched out in front of him and his great shoulders filling up the old chair, she realized what a huge bear of a man he was. Somehow she rarely thought about his size. Only when he heaved logs onto the truck that would take two normal men to lift or pitched hay bales as if they were empty boxes did she realize how strong he was. Usually she was just aware of his gentleness and deep, almost childlike shyness.

She gave him a hug and kissed him on his forehead. He was less than fifty, but already his black hair was greying. He opened his eyes and smiled up at her.

"I wasn't really sleeping," he said in his soft, deep voice. "I was just resting my eyes."

"Right, Pop," Nancy laughed. "If you'd been resting any harder you'd have shaken the porch down with your snores."

He reached up with his great hands and touched her cheek. "I didn't know if you were coming back this afternoon. I'm glad you did."

Nancy hugged him again. "Come on, Pop, help me with dinner. I stopped by Grebs' today and got some hamburger. We'll whip something up."

Her father sat still in the chair looking out over the clearing. Their small garden stretched almost to the end of the bench, where a fringe of trees marked the steep drop to the river. On their left they could see the wedge of mountains separating the two rivers.

"I love the spring," he said softly. "I love the smells, the green haze of new leaves." He pointed across the river. "The mountains are still snowy on top like they're blooming in great white blossoms."

They sat in silence for a few moments. Then Nancy got up and went back into the house. She paused by the shelves of jars, took down some tomatoes she'd canned last fall, and continued into the kitchen.

Her father came in a few minutes later with a pole and a carving knife. He sat at the table and worked at the pole. Nancy was struck once again by how delicately his big hands shaped the soft wood.

"How was school?" he asked without looking up from the carving.

Nancy thought briefly. "Well, it wasn't exactly the high point of my career." She went back to chopping onions.

Her father put down his knife and gave her a long look. "Nancy, I don't want you to give up now. You've come too far. When I was in residential school we couldn't go past grade eight. Between going to church in the morning and having to work in the fields after school for four hours a day, I didn't learn much even then. But things are different now. You can make it."

The onions stung Nancy's eyes. She wiped them with the back of her hand. "I'm not quitting Pop. I'll just be glad when it's over."

Her father returned to his work. "How did the rest of the day go?"

"I had a run-in with Grebs. He took Rita Thomas' cheque and only gave her $40 back. He can't do that."

"You didn't say anything, did you?"

Nancy slammed her knife down. "You're damned right I said something! And maybe if more people said something rather than moping or sitting around drinking themselves to death we might make some changes around here!"

The silence swept into the room like a cold northern wind. Nancy threw the onions into a frying pan and straightened up. Her voice softened.

"I'm sorry, Pop. I didn't mean you."

"Of course you did," her father replied. "And you're right." He paused. "I can't fight them. Their words...their certainty. They're all sharp edges and barbs. They're like great engines — full of power but with no spirit, no humanity. In the old days there were spirits here in the mountains that helped us find our strength. But they have even taken away the spirits."

Nancy looked up from the stove. Tears streamed down from his eyes. His hands were open and limp in his lap.

"Does the drinking make you feel stronger?" she asked softly.

"No." Her father spoke slowly, without anger or apology. "It just helps me forget what I've lost."

30

After dinner, Nancy slipped on her jacket and retraced her steps back to the ferry landing. The ferry was loading on the far side of the river, and she waited alone on the sandy shore. The only sound was the constant backdrop of the muttering river and the growing hiss of the wind storming up the canyon. Banks of clouds like grey cotton were being pushed by the wind as if to plug the narrow gap in the mountains.

Morgan Adams pulled up next to Nancy in his pickup and turned off the engine. Morgan lived eight miles north on a small farm. He was a friend of her father's and Nancy knew they were somehow related to his wife Emmeline.

"Evening, Nancy," Morgan said, sliding his head out of the cab. "Going into town?"

Nancy smiled and nodded.

"Want a ride?"

Nancy thought a few moments then shook her head. "I don't think so, Mr. Adams. I sort of feel like walking. Thanks anyway."

"Suit yourself, but from the look of those clouds you might get wet." He motioned up the river with his head.

The ferry, propelled by the swift current pushing against its pontoons, moved soundlessly and swiftly toward them. With a gentle bump, it eased up against the loading ramp and Maurice jumped quickly onto shore to lash the ferry securely to the dock.

As they waited to depart, Nancy looked along the far shore. The old residential school, set a hundred yards from the edge, loomed dark and massive in a broad clearing. Abandoned now, it still fascinated Nancy. She felt that if she could understand it, the attitudes behind it and the effects it had had on her father and the four generations of her people that had gone there, she could somehow make more sense of what was wrong now.

The ferry glided into the far dock and came to a stop with a slight jolt. Distracted, Nancy stumbled slightly, then turned to disembark. Morgan drove slowly by her and honked.

The ferry was about a mile from town, and the unpaved road ran up a steep hill to a wide bench that contained the residential school. Once the school had been red brick, but sometime in the past it had been painted white — to show who was in charge, the Indians joked. Now the paint was peeling and great patches of red were reappearing. The massive structure looked pathetic and forlorn in the early evening. Untended yard, ragged and reverting to weeds, ran up to the wide cement steps.

Nancy impulsively turned right down the circular drive and walked toward the enormous structure. The central section, four stories high with great double doors in the middle, was flanked by a wing on each side, set back slightly like huge, embracing arms. A hundred empty windows looked out blindly on the neglected lawn.

Reaching the steps, Nancy looked up at the great arching entranceway. "St. James Indian Residential School, 1904" was carved into a long block set high above the door. She sat and ran her hands over the cold cement, worn smooth by countless feet of Indian children. Her father and grandparents had told her about living here. They'd described how they had been uprooted from their family and community when they were five or six years old, and then were shipped to this harsh and alien place. Forced to put on dark uniforms, they'd been forbidden to speak their language and to follow the spiritual traditions of their people. Boys were separated from girls for eight years, and the nuns and priests who ran the place made every decision for them: when to sleep, get up, eat, work; what to wear, what to eat.

Nancy felt that old mix of anguish and rage again. How could they have done that? How could they treat us like animals? She thought of the children separated from their families for months. What did they return to? Strangers and shattered communities. What happened to the parents, their children taken? What a sense of helplessness, of loneliness they must have felt. Their subjection had become complete.

And how were the children supposed to learn the skills and responsibilities of being a parent? The old models were destroyed and there were no new ones to replace them. What about her own mother? She'd been young when Nancy was born, only eighteen. How could she have known how to be a proper mother? She'd left seven years later. She had just disappeared one day and not come back. But Nancy still remembered her warmth and laughter, as well as lying in bed awake listening to her mother crying. "I'm trapped here, Ben. I don't know who I am and I'm dying here."

Nancy stood up and looked once more at the monstrosity, paint flaking like scabs on old wounds. Then she turned and walked back toward the main road. Behind her, the school sank into the gathering gloom like an enormous haunted house. But the shadow of the place followed Nancy down the drive.

It was almost completely dark by the time Nancy got into town. What little twilight was left was being blotted out by dark clouds massing overhead. The wind kicked up in spurts and hurled a few raindrops in her face. As she came over the crest of the last hill Nancy could see streetlights in a row, and gusts of wind swirled dust and last year's leaves down Main Street. Nancy zipped her windbreaker up to her chin and walked past the long porch of the hotel. At the corner she turned right, passed by the cafe, and paused in front of the double doors in the stuccoed wall. Above her head, a garish neon sign in the shape of a wagon wheel flashed "Wag On Inn" at irregular intervals. Nancy shook her head and pulled the door open.

No matter how many times she entered, Nancy was always astonished when she walked into the pub. Since it had no windows, there wasn't the slightest suggestion outside of the noise and life that throbbed just inside the doors. The interior had once been some sort of phony western motif. The walls were panelled in rough boards and wagon wheels and ox yokes hung around the dim interior. Small round tables crowded close together were covered in stained and torn red terry cloth that matched the worn-out carpeting. A short bar was up against the left wall and a pool table hid in the gloom in the far right corner. A juke box near the door pumped out a constant stream of country and western music.

People sat huddled in small groups around tables laden with beer glasses. Some leaned back in their chairs, methodically working at their beer while they stared with empty eyes at the walls. The place was crowded as usual. Cowboys and would-be cowboys laughed noisily while young railroad workers jostled each other around the pool table. Indians sat in quieter groups. A few older couples sat silently in corners, drinking long since replacing conversation as the basis of their relationships. Sometimes occasional tourists wandered in. They sat wide-eyed against the walls, eyes darting nervously around the room, wondering what they had walked into. They rarely stayed long.

Underneath the smoke and din of laughter and conversation was a tremor of barely suppressed violence. Rarely a night went by without a fight erupting and rolling across the floor, chairs and bodies flying, beer glasses whizzing through the air to crash against the panelled walls. That's when Roy McAllister, the 6'3" bartender who scowled out from behind the bar, swung into action. With a white father and an Indian mother, Roy had absolutely no prejudice: he hated Indian and white equally and he liked nothing better than to rip some brawling Indian off a drunken cowboy, bash them both around a while, then throw them in a heap on the sidewalk outside.

Nancy spotted George and Barry sitting by themselves by the bar. She nodded to Roy on the way to the table, but he only glowered back at her. Nancy assumed he knew she was under age, but no one had ever questioned her, and she had been coming into the pub for years. When she was fifteen she had started routinely retrieving her father. She would often sit down to persuade him to leave, get involved in conversation and end up spending suppertime there. Maybe no one questioned her because Nancy never drank. She had realized early how simple it would be to slip into alcohol as a way of life, and she'd vowed then that she would never start. She had never broken that vow.

She slid into an empty chair next to George, leaned over, and gave him a kiss on the cheek.

George looked up brightly. "Well, things have certainly warmed up since this morning. Is this the beginning of a wild night of love?"

Nancy looked disgusted. "I'm just trying to apologize. I know I was a little distracted earlier."

"Distracted? Lady, you were in another galaxy millions of light years away."

"I know," Nancy said. "Things just seem to be getting to me. The bridge, school, my father, Grebs. This whole damned town is grinding me down, chewing me up. I just can't wait to get out of here."

George nodded toward Barry. "Yeah. I heard about Grebs. That guy's so cheap he charges extra for the pork fat in a can of beans."

"It's not just a matter of being cheap," Nancy replied. "He's draining us. It's not enough to steal what little money people have; he humiliates us in the process. We file through there like sheep, and every time we do we feel a little weaker, a little less in control. We make him rich while he makes us ashamed for letting him exploit us." Nancy ran her fingers through her hair. "I don't know."

"Yeah, well. Did you hear about the accident Danny Jones and Peter Adams got into?" George asked.

Nancy looked up in alarm. The two were men who worked with George. "Oh no, what happened?"

"Well, Danny's cousin was up from Vancouver, and they all piled into Danny's old pickup. You know his truck, what kind of shape it's in?"

Nancy and Barry nodded. Even in Creighton Danny Jones' truck was legendary. It was ancient, and it had so many body parts replaced with salvaged pieces of discarded trucks that no one could tell what make it was. The police routinely pulled it over every time Danny brought it across the river. Nancy and Barry leaned forward, concern on their faces.

"Danny and Peter were up front, and Danny's cousin got into the back. He was tired from the trip up, so he fell asleep on some hay." George paused and took a sip of beer. "They were headed up to Latham Lake to do some fishing, but when they got to that big hill above Four Mile — you know that long, steep one that dives almost down to the river?"

Nancy and Barry nodded again. "Yeah," Barry said impatiently. "So what happened, for God's sake?"

"Well, they started going down that long hill, and when they got to the first curve Danny hit the brakes. Nothing. No brakes. So here they were, careening down this hill, picking up speed to beat hell, and Peter yells, 'Hit the emergency brake.' Well Danny reaches under the dash, pulls on the lever, the old rusty cable snaps, and the whole thing comes off in his hand.

"Now they're going faster than ever and they're heading directly for that big rock face at the bottom of the hill. They're going like seventy miles an hour, and Peter yells, 'What are we supposed to do now?' 'Wake up my cousin,' Danny says. 'What good is that going to do?' Peter shrieks back. 'Well, nothing', says Danny, 'But he's from the city and he ain't never seen a wreck like the one we're going to have.'"

"Oh, geez," Nancy groaned, sitting back in her chair. "That's not funny, George," she said, "You had me scared. I thought you were serious."

Barry chuckled and drained his beer glass. He motioned toward the bar. "I see Laughing Boy is tending bar tonight. Maybe we should tell him to go home and rest up for the big game tomorrow night. He's pitching."

"You tell him," said George.

"What big game?" asked Nancy.

"You know, the Braves against the Cops and Teachers."

Nancy's eyes sparkled. "Is that tomorrow?" Both Barry and

35

George played for the Braves. There were three native teams, but the Braves were the elite. The others were like farm teams where a guy, over a period of years, could work his way into one of the rare vacancies that came up on the Braves. They played in a loose league, but the only games that really mattered were against the team of RCMP officers and teachers. No one could remember how the alliance between the teachers and police had begun, but it seemed somehow appropriate, and when they played the Braves the whole town turned out.

"Yeah," muttered Barry, his dark eyes going cold. "And we're going to kick ass. It's not many times we get a chance to beat the crap out of the cops. Usually it's the other way around."

Nancy was vaguely aware of something missing. The music box was silent, and an uneasiness seemed to fill the room. George shoved some quarters at Barry. "Go play a few tunes, Barry. And whatever you do, don't put on any of that awful country and western stuff. Find something that rocks a little."

Barry touched the front of his hair. "Right, Boss." He made his way toward the juke box, weaving around chairs and tables. He dropped in a bunch of quarters and punched a few buttons. A Dire Straits song came across the speaker and melded with the babble of voices.

A shout erupted by the pool table, and a drunk middle-aged railway hand pushed his way toward the juke box. He grabbed Barry by the shoulder and yanked him around. "Hey," he growled belligerently. "What kind of crap is that? Put some country on that machine or I will."

The corners of Barry's mouth dropped and his lips formed a grim line as he turned full to face the drunk. He was several inches shorter than his antagonist, but his wiry frame seemed to sing with tension as his eyes snapped cold and deep. Barry was not the right guy to push around.

"Oh, no," breathed George in the suddenly quiet room. "I've seen that look before."

So had Nancy. Barry was usually easy going and soft spoken, but he had a dark side, too, and it didn't take much to trigger it.

Even the drunk seemed to sense that he was picking more than a routine fight. He stumbled back a step and dropped his hands. Barry turned back slowly to the juke box.

"Thank God," sighed George, relaxing back into his seat.

Suddenly the drunk lunged at the back of Barry's neck. Barry seemed to sense him coming before the attacker had moved more than a few inches. Barry brought his right elbow up and pivoted, putting all his fury and strength into the arm. The elbow caught the drunk square on the temple with a dull thud that carried across the room. The drunk spun halfway around and crashed face first on the red carpet.

Barry seemed to go berserk. He finished his pivot and planted a vicious kick into the downed man's side. Although nearly unconscious, the drunk groaned and doubled up. Barry leapt on his back and grabbed his hair. He started slamming the man's face into the floor, once, twice. Blood was trickling from his nose.

Suddenly Roy McAllister was over the two men. His eyes were crackling as he grabbed Barry in a hammerlock around the neck. With a bellow, he wrenched Barry up to his feet. Barry managed to tear away and, still defiant, stood facing Roy, arm drawn back. Roy leaped forward, his massive fist ready to crash into Barry's face.

Then George, banging over chairs and tables, stuck an arm between the two. "Wait a minute Roy," he yelled, "take it easy. You don't want to hurt that right hand of yours, now do you? Big game tomorrow, remember?"

Roy grabbed Barry's shirt front with his left hand over George's arm, his right fist still cocked.

"Whoa, buddy," George continued soothingly. "Us Indians gotta stick together, right? Hey, we're all Braves here, right? Come on guys, you make up half the infield. What would it look like if the pitcher was out with a broken hand and the first baseman was out because he was dead?"

Roy seemed to relax a little. He let go of Barry's shirt, lowered his arm and grunted, "I want you guys out of here. Now."

The railroad worker moaned softly on the floor. Barry was slowly returning to his senses, and he let his hands drop to his sides. Nancy grabbed her jacket and started pushing him toward the door. George was patting Roy on the back. "We were just on our way, Roy, old pal. Take care of that arm. OK?" He gave Roy's huge biceps a gentle squeeze and waved as he backed out the door.

Barry was leaning against the wall, breathing heavily. George went up and looked at him. "You all right?"

Barry nodded.

"Good. Maybe sometime you can save *my* life."

Lightning crackled across the sky, followed almost instantly by thunder that rolled down the mountains. Rain, blown by the wind, stung their faces.

"Listen guys," Nancy said. "It's really been fun, but I have to go home. I want to get across the bridge before this storm breaks wide open."

George looked at her with concern. "Are you sure you don't want to stay at my place tonight? I don't like you going across that bridge at night."

Nancy laughed. "I've done it a hundred times. I'll make it tonight." She kissed him and gave him a hug. "But thanks. Some other time. You take care of the Brown Bomber over here."

She said good night and headed through town toward the bridge. She followed the tracks for a while, then stood on the first tie of the trestle. A lightning flash lit the expanse of bridge for a brief moment. She could see the far side a hundred yards away. Before she got there she had to pick her way across five hundred ties. They were too close to fall through, but in the dark a stumble could throw her over the edge. Her heart beat wildly as she looked at the two strips of steel that plunged outward into the darkness. She pulled her jacket across her shoulders and put her foot on the next wet, glistening tie. She prayed that a train wouldn't come. She would make it, but the terror that was always there waited on the bridge. She felt it creep up on her as she stepped farther and farther into the darkness until neither shore was visible. She couldn't even see the glimmer of the river beneath her feet.

The wind shrieked around the timbers, and the ties shuddered and shook as black emptiness stretched all around her. She felt herself teetering, falling. Panic seized her, and she quickly knelt on the ties.

Slowly the dizziness subsided. Desperate to get off the bridge, she half ran, half crawled through the battering wind and rain. After what seemed an eternity, she sensed trees and rocks around her. Then she felt the solid crushed stone beneath the ties. With her breath shuddering in and out, she almost sobbed in relief. A lightning bolt revealed the familiar path off to the right. Gratefully she headed into the trees toward her home.

V.

Nancy managed to struggle through school the next day without major incident. As soon as the last bell shrilled through the corridors, bringing all activity to an abrupt halt, she headed down the hill to meet George and Barry for supper before the game. She walked through town until she got to the Corral, a pizza restaurant and video arcade where many of the students gathered after school.

The Corral was crowded and noisy when she pushed through the door. Video games across the back wall were pinging, buzzing, and ricocheting as people lined up to watch and wait their turn. Nancy noticed Pat Antoine and a bunch of his blank-eyed buddies crowding around a video screen. Pat was savagely jabbing a button, releasing a machine gun chatter of white blips that darted across the screen while dodging alien space ships. She could hear him chatter excitedly across the room: "Got the sucker! I'm gonna nail this one. Gonna blast this one out of the sky!"

Nancy sat down at the counter. Elsie Jantzen, her head topped by a jaunty red cowboy hat, strolled casually up to take her order. Her apron showed a bronc rider on an exploding horse, smoke billowing out of its nostrils. Beneath, letters formed by a lasso rope read Corral Cafe.

Elsie's jaws worked a wad of gum. "Want anything to eat?" she asked.

"No thanks," replied Nancy. "Just bring me a Dr. Pepper." Barry had gotten her hooked on the darned things.

Elsie looked bored. "All we've got is Coke, 7-Up, and Orange."

"Okay. Make it a small Coke."

Elsie resumed chewing. "Last of the big spenders," she muttered.

Nancy sipped her Coke and looked around. A few people looked up and smiled or waved, but most seemed too involved in their video screens and cigarettes to notice her. Somehow the isolation and separation of the school had followed them down the hill. She opened up her English book. "When two or more ideas in a sentence are alike in function, they can and should be expressed in the same grammatical forms. For example, Midge wants to hop, skip, and jump."

Nancy snapped the book shut and pushed it aside. She just wasn't in the mood for parallel Midge today. Instead she opened her notebook. Inside, a poem was forming on a sheet of paper. She read the beginning.

This town has teeth
Not the sharp, shiny teeth
of a wolf
that tear and rip with quick slashes
or the mountains' teeth
that stand, bared in irregular rows
gleaming in the sunlight.
This town's teeth are big and white
like the dull molars of some large animal.
These teeth grind against each other,
slowly they crush...

A half hour later she was still engrossed in the poem when somebody suddenly clapped his hands over her eyes. She stifled a scream when she heard a falsetto voice behind her. "Guess who," it trilled.

"Tiny Tim," Nancy said, prying the fingers from her face. "George, why can't you just say 'Hi' like a normal person?"

George plunked himself on the stool beside her. "Listen," he hissed, "people have accused me of being a lot of things, but normal isn't one of them."

"With good reason," agreed Nancy.

Just then Barry walked through the door and stode over to Nancy and George. He grabbed George by the arm and punched him lightly on the shoulder.

"Just an hour away. You ready?"

"Geez," Nancy said in disbelief. "You sound like you're talking about getting married or going on national T.V. This is a baseball game."

"It's a baseball game to you," confided Barry, "but to us it's war!"

"Boys," mused Nancy. "Boys in men's clothing."

They ordered a quick pizza then headed up to the ball field. "Say," said George, "I've got a question for you. Why were Indians the first ones in Canada?"

"What's that supposed to mean?" asked Nancy. "We were first because we got here first."

"Just answer the question," said George, rolling his eyes in exasperation. "It's a joke."

"I should have known," Nancy muttered.

"I don't know," replied Barry dutifully. "Why were Indians the first ones in Canada?"

"Because we had reservations!" George grinned expectantly. "Get it?"

"George," Nancy said. "We don't even call them reservations up here. They're reserves. Indians have reservations in the States."

George looked hurt. "So it was adapted. Can't you use your imagination?" He looked from Nancy's unsmiling face to Barry, who seemed preoccupied. "Boy, you guys are a tough audience. By the way, thinking of baseball, did you ever wonder why they always name sports teams after Indians? There's the Washington Redskins and..."

"The Kansas City Chiefs," offered Barry.

"Yeah. How come they don't call themselves the Washington White Boys or something?"

Nancy snorted in amusement, but Barry gave a short, bitter laugh. "They name their teams after Indians because we're not quite human," he said. "We're sort of on the same level as bears, lions, devils, blue jays, pirates, that sort of thing. We're mascots."

"But you guys call yourselves the Braves," protested Nancy. "What's the difference?"

"We're Indians — that's the difference," Barry retorted. "We can call ourselves the Braves because we *are* the Braves. When some whites do it they're putting us right in there with the birds and beasts."

"Yeah," mused George. "When I buy *my* baseball team I'm going to turn the tables. I can see it now: the Cleveland Caucasians."

When they arrived at the ball field most of the players were already there. The Braves milled around the backstop while the RCMP and teachers warmed up. Most of the players were cops; big, thick men with powerful arms and neatly trimmed hair and mustaches. Their pitcher, Constable Thiessen, stood smiling on the mound. He exuded the confidence of a man accustomed to having others defer to him and his position.

Thiessen hurled a final ball into the catcher's mitt then waved the others in. "Come on guys. Let's give the Injuns a chance to loosen up. They'll need it."

On the way in he flipped the ball to a glowering Roy McAllister, who on nights like this knew where he fit on the colour line. "Here,

Chief," Thiessen said, "Be sure you give it back after the game, eh?"

Roy snatched the ball and took a step forward. Thiessen laughed. "Better control him, boys. We wouldn't want to have to arrest him for assault, would we?"

The Braves warmed up quietly, almost sullenly. There was no joy in this game. It was a grudge match.

The game started, and the Braves dominated in the early innings. They couldn't match the physical education teachers and muscled cops for sheer athletic ability and power, but they played with a grim determination and quickness that made up for any physical disadvantage. And besides, they had Roy McAllister pitching.

For the first few innings he was unhittable. He blazed ball after ball by the grunting cops. The few balls that were hit were slow grounders and the infielders, working like the parts of an intricate machine, had no trouble throwing every hitter out at first. By the fourth inning not a single player had advanced past third.

Thiessen was also pitching well, but the Braves were hitting him. In the third, George lined a solid triple over the left fielder's head and Buddy Adams knocked him in with a clean single. In the next inning Barry led off with a single. This was followed by a walk. Then Thiessen got the next two men out. Roy came to the plate. He lashed the first pitch into deep centre field. Two runs scored, but Roy tried to stretch the hit into a home run. Despite his size, he was fast, and he rumbled around third like a sprinting bear. The catcher blocked the plate, so Roy slammed into him just as the ball arrived.

The umpire, a young Indian from another team, hesitated. Thiessen charged in from pitcher's mound screaming, "Out! He was out!" and the catcher picked himself up and rushed toward the umpire waving the ball in his face and yelling, "I got him! Are you blind?"

The umpire caved in. "Out," he muttered. Roy leaped to his feet and started for the umpire, who was backing toward the fence. George and the other players grabbed Roy by the arms.

"OK," soothed George, "It's OK. We'll get 'em. Don't get thrown out of the game."

Roy was finally led back to the bench, and Thiessen and his catcher traded winks. Thiessen chuckled as he walked back to the mound to pick up his glove.   ·

The Braves emerged from the inning with a three-run lead, but something seemed to have snapped. McAllister threw more fiercely than ever, but without control. Then he began to tire. The cops started to hit him. The fielding became more ragged. Balls were missed; throws were wide or slow; runs began to score.

In the stands Nancy watched in anguished disbelief. "What's wrong with you guys?" she screamed. But then she too subsided into a dull silence. A sense of resignation seeped from the players into the Indian spectators. At the same time, the cops and teachers became more cocky.

The taunts became louder and more raucous. "McAllister drinks too much beer to go beyond three innings! These guys can't hit anyone who isn't drunk! What's the matter? Your ponytail gettin' in the way?"

The game ended at last. The Braves had lost nine to three. The white players pounded each other on the back, climbed into their cars, and sped off. The Braves hung around dejectedly before drifting off one by one.

Nancy sat alone in the stands. The sun had set and the sky was getting dark. Barry and George walked over and sat near her.

"What happened to you guys?" blurted Nancy. "You just gave up."

Barry pounded his fist into his mitt distractedly. "We'll get 'em next time," George said brightly. "It's early in the season. We just haven't hit peak form yet."

Suddenly Barry slashed a vicious punch into his mitt and cursed. "Nancy's right. We gave up. We stopped playing. We just gave them the game."

"No, Barry," George began, "that's not..."

Barry turned on him angrily. "We did, George, and you know it. And you know why? Because we're losers. Because we're so used to losing that we don't know how to win. And once we thought we might lose again, we stopped trying." Barry's voice was taut with intensity. "That way we can say, 'It didn't matter. We didn't really try anyway.' But it does matter. It *does* matter."

There was a long silence. The dark dropped like a blanket around their shoulders.

"Let's have a beer," George said at last.

The three stood up and headed along the road toward the pub. No one said anything as they walked. The ball park was located in a field next to the elementary school, and the walk into town took them through an area of trees and brush. The street was deserted and the night was utterly silent.

Suddenly they heard a muffled scream. Nancy, George, and Barry stopped simultaneously, their ears straining. Now they could hear low voices and the sound of a struggle in the bushes off to their left.

George waved Nancy back. "You stay here," he said. "Barry and I will go see what's going on."

"No way, George. I'm coming too."

George hesitated, then shrugged. The three of them pushed cautiously through the leaves and branches toward an old ponderosa pine that grew out of the underbrush. As they neared the tree, the voices became more distinct. There seemed to be four or five people speaking in low, harsh tones.

"Damn it!" one cried. "She bit me!"

"Hold the bitch," another voice snarled. "And hurt her if you have to." A sharp slap cracked through the night and there was a woman's stifled cry.

"Keep your hand over her mouth!" hissed another male voice. "Listen," it continued. "We're gonna show you who's boss, and the more you struggle the more we'll hurt you. Understand?"

Nancy felt her fingers dig into George's arm. They stood just a few feet away now. The thrashing and struggling seemed to have subsided.

"That's better," the voice continued. Nancy thought it sounded familiar, but the night was whirling around her and she couldn't be sure. She heard a zipper, then the tinkle of a belt buckle.

"Hurry up," urged another voice, "or we'll be here all night."

George suddenly tore from Nancy's grip. "What's going on here?" he bellowed. At the same time he lunged through the bushes toward the tree. Nancy followed close behind.

There was a chorus of curses and the noise of scrambling feet. "Someone's coming. Let's get out of here!"

George and Nancy burst through the fringe of bush into a small clearing underneath the tree. Young men were spilling into the underbrush on all sides. But one, hampered by his pants still around his ankles, was still in the clearing. He looked up, terror written across his young face as he desperately tried to pull up his jeans.

Nancy stared in numbed shock. It was Pat Antoine.

Then he too scurried into the bushes. Now they saw the girl lying on her side, trying to cover herself with her torn clothes. She was

44

sobbing quietly.

Nancy saw it was Lucy Jack, who lived on the reserve next to Nancy's grandmother. Lucy couldn't have been more than sixteen. Nancy knelt down and put her arm around Lucy's shuddering shoulders. She hugged her, rocking back and forth slowly until the sobs subsided. "Are you OK?" Nancy asked softly.

Lucy nodded her head, never looking at them. She stood up shakily, tucking in her shirt and trying to brush off the dirt. Her face, wet with tears, shone in the moonlight.

Nancy stood with her, holding her arm. "Do you want to go to the hospital?"

Lucy shook her head. "I'm all right."

"Well, let's get you down to the RCMP then."

For the first time Lucy looked up. Fear lit her eyes. "I can't go to the cops," she said quickly.

"What do you mean you can't go to the cops?" Nancy asked. "They tried to rape you! Are you just going to let them get away with that?"

Lucy shook her head miserably. "They were friends. One's even a cousin. If I turned them in no one would ever talk to me again. Anyway, the cops wouldn't believe me. I'm not going into some court room and have some lawyer tear me apart."

Nancy's eyes blazed. Her voice quickened with anger. "So you let them off scott free so they can assault another woman, or maybe even you, or me, some other night. Look, George and I and..." she looked around for Barry. "George and I will back up your story. How are we going to stop this if no one will press charges?"

Lucy shook her head. "I'm sorry, Nancy. I can't do it. I'm..." her shoulders began to shake again. "I'm afraid."

"I know," Nancy said softly. "I'm sorry too, Lucy." Nancy put her arm around Lucy's shoulders again. "Let me walk you home."

"No," Lucy said, her voice quavering. "I just live over there. I'll be OK."

"You sure?" Nancy asked.

"Yeah, really. I'd rather be alone. And listen," Lucy looked up at both of them, her soft brown eyes shining with tears, "thanks". She left the clearing and made her way back to the road. Nancy watched her as she walked toward her house.

"Damn," sighed Nancy. "Damn it, George! They're going to get away with it."

George shrugged. "I guess so."

"Who would *do* something like that?" she raged. "What's wrong with people?"

George put his arms around her, and they hugged each other tightly. Nancy clung to him for a moment, then began pounding his back in fury. "George," she whispered fiercely, "we've got to get out of here."

"Right now let's get to the pub," he said gently.

Nancy looked around. "Where's Barry?"

"I don't know." George looked puzzled. "I thought he was right behind us."

They walked back to the road. Barry stood in the shadows twenty feet away, his face hidden. George and Nancy approached him.

"Barry," Nancy said as she neared him. "What happened? We thought..." She faltered. He turned toward her, and she could see tears on his face. "Barry, what's wrong?"'

Barry dragged a sleeve fiercely across his eyes. "Nothing," he murmured. "I'm OK."

George was with them now. "Let's go for that beer," he suggested, his voice tired and flat. "I need it."

They walked the short distance to the pub and found a table in a corner. Barry kept his face down, buried in his hands.

"Barry," Nancy began, "what happened to you back there?"

There was a long silence. "I don't know. I guess I got scared."

Nancy decided to let it drop. Barry often withdrew into himself, reliving old hurts, licking old wounds. The best thing to do was to leave him to himself until he came out of it.

She turned to George, "I just don't understand. Why would anyone do that? What sort of scum would gang rape a sixteen-year-old girl?"

"Scum like me," Barry blurted out. He lifted his face up slowly. Agony and pain twisted his features. "Scum like me," he said more softly.

"What do you mean?" Nancy asked. The noise of the pub receded, and she was aware only of Barry's tortured face.

"You see," Barry said slowly. "I've been there before. Not once. Several times. Years ago now, but tonight it all came back. I'd tried to shut it all out, deny it. The screams, the struggling. The shame. But tonight it was like a terrible dream that returns after you think it's forgotten forever."

"But why, Barry. Why would you do it?" cried Nancy.

Barry looked her full in the face.

"Because for one moment, for a few seconds, you feel powerful. Nobody is slapping you around. Nobody is making you feel small and weak. For one minute you're in control." His eyes softened with tears and his voice faltered. "But then, after it's over, only the shame remains. And the terrible weakness. Knowing you're trying to cure your own weakness with someone else's pain. Knowing you are lessening yourself, becoming part of the forces destroying us."

The tears now ran slowly down his cheeks. "And that's when you begin to hate yourself for your weakness, for what you're doing to your women, to your people, to yourself. But the weaker you feel the more you want to stop the pain. And every day you see again how powerless you are. In the schools there are the teachers and the meaningless crap they tell you to learn. And in the streets there's the cops telling you what you can and can't do. Who owns the stores? This hotel? The pub? They're all white. And you see your people dying around you and you know you can't do anything and that you're going nowhere. So you do it again. And for a few minutes you feel powerful again."

Barry's voice trailed off and his eyes fixed on the table in front of him. His fingers were tangled in his thick black hair. With the back of his hand, he tried to stop his nose from running. Her eyes stinging with tears, Nancy dug into her jacket pocket and fished out a piece of Kleenex. She passed it to him. Then she reached over and touched his other hand.

"I'm sorry, Barry," she whispered. "I really am."

Barry tried a small smile. "So am I. So am I."

VI.

School seemed even more meaningless than usual the next day. Nancy's mind kept drifting back to the incident the night before. She usually enjoyed math — its clean, secure world of absorbing absolutes, formulas, and numbers at least provided a respite from the agonizing boredom of other classes, boredom that forced her to turn to the questions and bewildering uncertainty that surrounded her. But today not even math could untrack her as she tried to make sense out of what had happened.

It wasn't that she had been unaware — from rumours and overheard boasts, she had known about the assaults for a long time. But it had never affected her directly. Now she felt that to just sit by would be like accepting it all, adding to the climate of helplessness and despair. But what could she do, especially since Lucy wasn't even willing to press charges?

And what was she to make of Barry's revelations? Just about the time she was ready to consider the whole thing the action of a few sick punks, one of her best friends admitted to having done the same thing. It seemed as though the world had turned on its head.

By lunch she knew she had to do something. She simply couldn't stand the rage that filled her. If Lucy and other victims wouldn't act, at least she had to confront the one rapist she'd recognized — Pat Antoine.

Pat was in grade nine. Grade nine, she thought. Even though he'd failed twice, he was still only about sixteen. She walked down the hall toward his English class and waited by the door. The rest of the students streamed into the hall, but Pat wasn't among them. Finally she poked her head in the room and saw Pat sitting and looking sulkily at the floor. His English teacher, Mr. McNamara, a young, earnest man with longish hair, stood over him.

"Now, Pat," he said, his voice reasonable but firm, "what was the idea of throwing spitballs? Do you think that's acceptable behavior in a classroom? And what about the other students who want to listen? Were you being fair to them?"

Pat remained silent and sullen. A sneer twisted his lips.

McNamara, clearly forcing himself to be patient and unruffled, continued. "I don't know what your problem is and I don't care, but you've been surly all year and I've just about had enough. If you can't be cooperative and considerate in here, I'm quite prepared to see you get your walking papers. Understand?"

Pat stood up suddenly, erupting in McNamara's face. The teacher started to put a hand to his shoulder as if to push him back into his seat, but Pat brought his fist around sharply and knocked McNamara's hand away. Now he met McNamara's stare, his eyes glittering perilously.

McNamara took a step back.

"Yes, well," he faltered. "I think we understand each other now. You may go."

The teacher walked quickly to the front of the room where a white girl waited patiently by his desk. "Ah, Jeanette," he beamed. "You wanted some help on the story we read in our reader. Well, it's a chapter from *Little House on the Prairie*. Do you know that book?"

The girl nodded while Pat picked up his books and moved toward the door.

"Yes, good," McNamara continued. "Well, it's a story about responsibility. Laura and her family have moved to Indian country, and Laura is in charge of the cattle. But she forgets to close the gate, right?"

Pat was almost at the door before he saw Nancy. At first his face went blank with fear and surprise, but it quickly resumed its sullenness. He shouldered her out of the way and stepped into the hall. All Nancy's confusion and uncertainty turned to rage as he tried to push by her. She grabbed his shoulder and shoved, slamming him against the lockers. Once more fear lit up his eyes, and Nancy realized how young he was. She almost felt pity for him. Then his eyes turned hard.

"Get out of my way. You can't prove nothin'," he muttered.

"Listen," she said fiercely, "Lucy doesn't have to press charges, you know. I can." She didn't know if this was true, but it sounded good.

"Sure," he scoffed, "and you're gonna get a long way if she refuses to testify. Give me a break."

"You slime," she said. She looked in his face, closed and hard, and felt anger and fear. "How can you gang-rape girls and feel nothing? What's wrong with you, Pat? What the hell's *wrong* with you?"

Pat took a step toward her, pushing his face into hers. "Don't get on my case, cousin," he sneered, "or you could be the next one."

Nancy never knew where the punch came from, but she felt it start

50

deep down inside her and coil in her arm. She felt the arm swing silently, swiftly upward, her hand closed tight into a fist. She felt the knuckles crash into Pat's temple, and she saw the expression of pain and astonishment flash across his face before he crumpled to the floor, his books spilling around him.

Pat scrambled to his feet quickly, and Nancy stepped back, her fists raised. She'd seen enough fights to know how to handle herself, and a cold rage pushed out any fear. His face twisted in hatred, Pat cocked his arm.

Suddenly a huge hand reached out from behind Pat and grabbed his wrist just before he could bring his fist hurtling toward Nancy.

"I should smash your face in for picking on girls," growled Mark Bateman, twisting Pat's arm back until he had him pinned against the lockers. "But that pleasure will have to wait until later."

Mark jerked his arm backwards, throwing Pat into a heap on the hall floor. The younger boy picked himself up and glowered at the two of them, then scuttled around picking up his books and fled down the hall, still glaring at them with hatred.

Nancy was shaking. She put a hand on the locker to steady herself. Mark turned toward her. "You all right?"

"Yeah," Nancy said. "And thanks, Mark."

Mark stood up straight again. His eyes were a little too close together and they had a way of glowing with self-importance. "I think that's the first nice thing you've ever said to me," he preened.

"I think that's the first nice thing you've ever done," retorted Nancy.

"What was that all about, anyway?" Mark asked. "A little intertribal warfare?"

"Geez, Mark. It's too bad you're such a jerk. I'd really like to try to be civil to you, but you make it so hard."

Mark looked stricken. "Listen, I just saved you from Chief Crazy Horse and that's the thanks I get. What's wrong with you Indians, anyway?"

Nancy looked at him in amazement. She jabbed her finger in his chest. "Look Mark, when your sailors, hopelessly lost, stumbled onto us, thinking they'd found India, your ancestors were living in stone huts. One in ten was deformed because of malnutrition. Most of you lived in a state of near slavery. Your church was in the middle of torturing and executing millions of people because they thought a little differently. When you got here you were kept alive by our generosity. You repaid that by attacking our religious traditions, stealing our land and killing three-quarters of us with your diseases. There's nothing wrong with us that you haven't created."

Nancy turned and stalked off down the hall. Mark stood paralyzed against the lockers, his mouth partially open. Finally he shook his head. "Touchy, touchy," he mumbled.

All afternoon Nancy was in a complete daze, and as a result she was more thankful than usual that she ended the day with a double home economics block. She could slip into the routine and lose herself in group efforts without having to worry about being singled out to perform.

But Bernice didn't miss much. Halfway through the first period she came over to the counter where Nancy was quietly measuring ingredients into a bowl. She watched silently for a while, looking as closely at Nancy's face as at the recipe. "You doing OK?" Bernice asked softly.

Nancy kept her eyes on the bowl. "I'm all right."

Bernice nodded. "OK, but if you want to talk, you know where I am."

Nancy looked at her and smiled her thanks.

Bernice reached over and squeezed her hand. "I mean it," she said. Then she walked to where Jacob Worabey was struggling with cake ingredients.

After school Nancy found herself walking through town toward Barry's. She wasn't exactly sure why, but something bothered her about the night before. Barry's confessions, of course, but there was something else, something about the tears and the terrible pain and bitterness that had coloured his words. She wanted to talk with him, take away the hurt, wash away the memories. She wanted to close the wounds that were bleeding him to death.

Barry lived on the reserve in an old plywood house that was the colour of dried blood. He had inherited it when his father died and his mother moved in with Barry's sister. It was so poorly built that the cheap sliding windows wouldn't close, and Barry had stuffed rags in the gaps to keep out bugs and the cold. The front door too was jammed shut, so the only entrance was through the back. As Nancy walked around the house, she noticed how the plywood was pulling away from the studs and how the cement foundation was cracking. The Department of Indian Affairs had built them as cheaply as it could. No wonder they self-destructed in twenty years or burned like tinder boxes when the hastily installed wiring shorted in the walls or the cheap metal chimneys caught on fire. There had been six house fires in the past two years. Five people had died.

Barry's car was parked alongside the house, so Nancy walked up the single step to the back door, which was stained dark brown from rain and use. Knocking softly at first, she decided to pound when there was no response. With still no answer, she twisted the door knob. Immediately the door popped open and she walked into the kitchen.

Nancy had expected to find stacks of unwashed dishes piled in the sink as usual and bags of garbage in the corners, but everything was neat and in place. Dishes were clean and stacked on the shelves. Surprised and beginning to worry for no reason she could quickly identify, she walked into the living room at the front of the house. The inexpensive stereo sat on the milk crates Barry had borrowed permanently, his few records stacked inside. The old chesterfield, worn and frayed, sat against the wall. She poked her head into the first bedroom, where Barry made his arrowheads and stored his tools, but it too was empty. Barry's bedroom had a single mattress pushed up against a wall. Nancy stared. The sheets and blankets were pulled up and carefully smoothed over the pillow.

Becoming more and more agitated, Nancy rushed to make sure Barry wasn't in the bathroom. But the door was open and the small room was empty. She walked slowly out the back and pulled the door closed.

She headed back downtown, hoping she would see George. She spotted his truck in front of the pub and walked over. She almost ran into him as he hurried out the door. Instinctively at first, then with affection, he held up his hands and put them on her shoulders.

"Hi. Have you seen Barry?" George asked, his face drawn and serious.

"No. I just went over to his house. His car was there but he wasn't. George," Nancy hesitated. "Is something wrong?"

A trace of a smile returned. "Naw. He just seemed a little down last night and I wanted to cheer him up."

Nancy became more concerned. "George, I've been with you long enough to know when you're lying. What's going on."

"It's probably nothing," George said, tugging distractedly at his ponytail. "He was just, he kept saying things like he didn't know how much longer he could take it and that sort of thing. We went over to

53

his house after the pub closed and I stayed with him until about four this morning. He'd cry for a while then lash out, smashing the walls until his knuckles were bleeding. Finally he seemed to calm down. He said he wanted to sleep and told me to go home." George rubbed his forehead. "Now I wish I hadn't."

"Why?" Nancy asked in alarm. "Has something happened?"

"No, no. Everything's fine, I'm sure. I just wish I could find him."

They walked together toward the truck. "Let me give you a ride home," George said.

"No, I can walk down to the ferry. You go look for Barry."

"Yeah, OK. Maybe he's just walking up in the hills. He does that sometimes when he's upset. I'll see you later."

George got into the old pickup. It shuddered to life, and he leaned out the window and waved before pulling out from the curb. Nancy hugged her books to her chest and began the long walk.

That night she was quiet. She was almost relieved when the ferry closed, and for one of the few times in her life she was grateful that they didn't have a phone. She didn't want to think about Barry, but she couldn't think about anything else. She and her father sat on the back porch in silence long into the soft spring night. She could see his cigarette burning in the dark like a single eye.

She slept little during the night, and early the next morning, Nancy heard what she'd dreaded most: the sound of an old truck creaking and rattling down the drive. She was up and at the door before George reached the front porch. His eyes seemed sadder, his face more drawn than she'd ever seen them before.

Nancy opened the screen door and ran to him. He hugged her fiercely, digging his fingers into her back. Then, as if to hide from some terrible knowledge, he buried his face in her shoulder.

"Come on in," Nancy said softly. "I'll make some coffee."

George walked through the door and sat on a chair by the kitchen table. He held his forehead in his left hand, elbow braced on the table. "They found him," George said softly. "His body washed up down river. Near Parson's Landing."

Nancy thought she was prepared, but the words seemed to be strangely muffled. She went numb while her hands mechanically measured coffee.

"Someone said they saw him walking toward the bridge early yesterday morning."

The tears were beginning to well in her eyes now, but somehow she still managed to fill the coffee pot with water and set it on the stove. That done, she put her hands on the counter. She couldn't look at George.

"Did he jump?" she asked.

George was silent for a long time. Finally she glanced at him. He looked empty and weary. He shrugged his shoulders. "What do you think?" he asked softly.

VII.

Barry's body was taken to his house the next day and the wake lasted through the weekend. Women from the community came to clean the house, but they found little do to: Barry had cleaned his house the morning before his death. Nothing was out of place. Elders from the community took turns sitting by the open casket for the three nights of the wake, while a fire was kept burning outside by the road the entire time.

Nancy approached the house with dread. Many funerals, especially those for elders, were not times of great sadness. People came from hundreds of miles to honour the deceased and there was almost a sense of celebration, sharing and community. At times like these, the people found solace in their perseverance, their unity, their strength as a people despite everything.

But this time Nancy felt only emptiness and loss, and the familiar, hated feelings of confusion, bewilderment, and anger that were beginning to solidify in her stomach.

It was early morning, and the sun hung low and dull over the mountain that bulked up beyond the reserve and between the two rivers. The thin rays of light did little to dispel the chill in the air, and as Nancy approached the house three men stood close to the small fire they had tended all night. They spoke quietly and looked up briefly as she turned into the house.

The open casket lay on two chairs at one end of the room. Flowers were arranged around it and four women sat in chairs on each side of the casket. They had their heads bowed, and old Bessie Adams was speaking very quietly in Shuswap. Nancy stopped and bowed her head. These were the morning prayers. She listened to the voice chanting its ancient language, and, unable to understand a word, she became filled with a terrible sadness which swept through her like a cold wind from the mountains. Dizzy, she reached out to steady herself on the wall. She wanted to run away, to go and hide beneath a big pine tree, to lie on its bed of soft brown needles and to cry and cry. She wanted to be alone, to be anywhere but here.

The voice stopped and a new one began. This one chanted in a new language. Slowly she realized it was saying Hail Marys in flat, inflectionless English. Finally it too stopped. Then there was silence.

Nancy's head slowly cleared and she eased herself down onto the brown couch along the wall. One of the women came and sat down by her, silently taking Nancy's hand in her own. Nancy felt its warmth, the skin soft but tough like thin parchment.

She looked up gratefully. "I'm OK now. I just got a little dizzy."

She stood up and walked to the casket. At first she felt nothing. The grey, puffy face against the white satin lining wasn't Barry. It was something that looked vaguely like him, modeled out of lifeless vinyl and clay. And where did they get that ridiculous tie? Barry had never worn a tie in his life. The torso and head lay motionless on the satin bed. No subtle breath expanded the chest; no movement flickered around his lips or his closed eyelids. He was utterly and absolutely still.

The moan seemed to come from a secret corner. She didn't feel it coming, and it seemed that it was wrenched out of her, ripped from deep inside. Falling to her knees to escape the terrible certainty of the corpse, she sobbed uncontrollably, her face buried in her hands. The women gathered around her and gently touched her shoulders. Then, when it was time, they helped her back to the couch, where Bessie remained to stroke her hair and to hold her like a child while humming softly.

Nancy let herself be held. She rocked slowly back and forth and tried to speak between her sobs. "There's so much sadness," she stammered. "So much loss."

Bessie hummed for a few moments. "Yes," she said in slow, soothing tones. "Yes, so much sadness. But like the river, we're still here. We're still here."

They rocked rhythmically for a long time. Gradually Nancy's sobs slowed and the shaking stopped.

She looked up into deep brown eyes that shone like polished hazelnuts set in a softly creased face lit by a small, secret smile. How old was Bessie? Fifty, a hundred, three hundred years?

Nancy smiled tentatively back. Squeezing the old woman's hand she stood up uncertainly and looked around. Other people had come in to pay their respects, to share their sorrow. She looked again at the ancient face peering up at her, and she felt calm. With a smile of gratitude she walked slowly back through the kitchen and out the door.

The burial was held on Monday afternoon. At noon she left school and walked down the hill toward the house. Though most of the students knew or were related to Barry, the school remained in session, and only a few of his closest relatives came along. They joined others funneling toward Barry's house until several hundred stood in the yard and in the house.

A pickup was waiting at the back door. George and five other men carried the casket out, lifting it carefully onto the truck. Children carrying the flowers that had been arranged around the casket during the wake emerged from the house and lined up behind. Slowly the procession started off toward the church.

George walked beside the truck, and Nancy let herself be swept along in the silent river of people. They walked slowly up the gravel road, and the only sound was the crunch of shoes and the soft cry of a baby. The procession streamed back from the truck for fifty yards, and Nancy saw friends, elders, relatives, and children whom she recognized from other Shuswap communities. Together they surged toward the church, a great current of people, and Nancy was carried along like driftwood.

They filed into the little church until there was no more room and the rest stood patiently outside. The priest, who divided his time between the big white church a half mile away and the much humbler Indian church on the reserve, would be officiating as he usually did on special occasions.

Suddenly he bustled in from a side door, still adjusting his robes. Seeming a little peeved that he had had to interrupt his day for the service, he stood behind the pulpit, never glancing at the casket in front of him, and leafed through the hymnal.

"Ah, turn to page six for the service," he said briskly. Nancy picked up the book in front of her and flipped to the worn pages of the funeral service.

"We are here today," the priest read, "to mourn the passing of, uh, let's see..." In the book there was a line with the words "enter name of deceased" in brackets. "Ah yes, to mourn the passing of Barry Paul and to commend his soul to the care of..."

The priest read on, but the words were empty and brittle. People shuffled their feet impatiently and waited for the service to end. At last the pages and the priest ran out of words. The casket was reclaimed by the six pall bearers and carried back down the aisle and outside to the waiting pickup as the church bell slowly rang.

The building emptied and people began following the truck down the last quarter mile of the gravel road to the Indian graveyard, a flat, sandy rectangle that crept into the pines and hills surrounding the reserve. At its western edge it fell steeply toward the river below. Wooden and metal crosses with names carved and lettered by hand rose from the thick weeds and grass. Nearer the road there were newer mounds of dirt, some with crosses still hung with faded plastic flowers, and just inside the fence that ran along the road there was a row of six or seven graves only months old. Unsoftened by grass, they lay like raw wounds in the sod.

At the end of the row was an empty hole, fresh dirt piled high along one side. The truck pulled up beside the fence and the pallbearers slid the casket off the back. A crowd came together around the casket at the edge of the grave as old women in long drab dresses swayed slowly and dabbed at their eyes. Behind them, the church bell was still ringing.

And still they kept coming, elders, young people, children holding flowers, babies in their mothers' arms. Finally the priest arrived. He muttered a few words and fluttered around the casket like a white moth, but no one paid much attention. This was not his place.

Nancy looked at the faces of the people around her; faces set deep in sorrow, with eyes like stones. Then she looked over their heads to the river churning below and to the mountains that rose silent and white beyond the river's edge.

An elder stepped forward. His voice, though low and quiet, carried strongly through the crowd. He spoke at first in Shuswap, then in English.

"Barry was a young man, and it makes me sad to see such a one go to the spirit world. We have buried too many of our young people. But Barry was a good man. He cared for his people. He hoped for so much. Now he is at peace, but we must comfort each other, for his loss is a loss to us all. Let us ask the Creator to give us strength. Let us carry Barry's hopes and vision in our heart."

He stepped back and another man carrying a hand drum came forward. He began to beat the drum slowly and started a Shuswap chant. He was joined by the elders, and together their voices rose in a piercing, wavering keen. For a moment the ancient voices and this ancient song were all there was, shimmering hauntingly in the air. They were old like the mountains, like the river that flowed constantly from no origin to no end. This was the only moment, and it flowed backwards and forwards a thousand years.

Nancy was aware only of the chant, the drum beating in time with her heart, and the two hundred people around her who had merged into one. The song was an electrical current flowing through them, binding them. She felt her hands clasping four hundred other hands, her heart beating with two hundred hearts.

She couldn't tell how long the song continued. Was it just minutes? The spell still hung in the air like smoke as the drum began to beat a little faster and her voice rose with the voices of all the others. The chant of the honour song rolled across the cemetery, spilling over the edge into the river and ascending into the air, vibrating the sharp needles of the pines.

Then that too was over. The coffin was lowered into the grave on taut brown ropes. The bell, still tolling, seemed far away as the casket settled to the bottom. Then the bell stopped, and there was a new silence.

One by one the people began to come forward, taking a handful of dirt, throwing it on the casket, then turning away. Nancy was borne forward, and she found herself stooping to take some soil from the pile at the edge of the grave. Handfuls of dirt rained down from all sides, and the cheap white and gold top of the coffin was dusted in sand. She opened her hand and let its contents scatter on the casket. For a second it almost seemed that she touched Barry, and in that second she said goodbye. A great swelling in her throat made swallowing hard as she turned away.

She looked around, and it was like waking from a dream. The throng separated again. Next to her Sarah Paul, Barry's sister, stood weeping quietly. Nancy held her and they cried together. Friends, uncles, aunts, cousins, and strangers hugged them, smiled sadly at them, touched them tenderly, saying nothing.

Nancy turned back toward the grave where George and several other men were taking turns shovelling the remaining sand into the hole. This part of Barry's farewell was over, and now women from all over the community would be bringing food in pots and aluminum foil-covered pans to his house for a feast. Nancy longed to stay and be with them, to help them, draw strength and comfort from them, but she had only been excused from school for two hours. She had to go back for the rest of the afternoon. However, she knew the dinner would go on till evening, and afterwards they'd be playing stick games all night or even longer. She would be back.

She patted Sarah's arm then turned away. Nancy felt no need to wipe away the tears that streamed down her face. She walked slowly with the crowd back down the road, past the church, past Barry's old red house. People split away in small groups, and soon she was alone. As she passed through the town and trudged silently up the hill toward the school, her head felt heavy, and she heard only her own breathing. Unaware of the cars growling by her, or the sun and the soft wind that shook the sunflowers, she continued on, while her feet moved on their own, somehow staying between the asphalt and the drop-off to the river.

Suddenly, she was startled to find herself at the school door. She walked into the dark, cool lobby and glanced automatically at the clock — 1:45. Biology period. She walked into the office and picked up the pile of books she'd left there, not even noticing Doughnut's baleful glare. She numbly wandered down the hall to her classroom and opened the door. With a shock she realized she was in Quigley's class.

He whirled on her as she edged toward her seat, his little eyes aflame. "What's your excuse this time, Antoine?" he snarled. "You'd better have a late pass!"

Nancy stood motionless by her desk. Her mouth worked as she tried to explain but nothing came out. She stood looking at him, pleading. "Don't... don't," she stammered.

Her vulnerability seemed to inflame him. "Am I to infer from your unintelligible reply that you have neither excuse nor late pass?" he yelled.

Nancy looked at him uncomprehendingly. The rest of the class disappeared and there was only Quigley's veined face and tiny eyes. His lips twisted in anger.

"Can't you talk, Miss Antoine?" he raged. "I'm asking you a question!" His fury mounted as Nancy stood silently, desperately, trying to make the words come. "What's wrong with you people?" he spat. "You can't tell time and you can't even explain yourselves. You just stand there with a blank expression on your face. Your mouth is moving, but all that comes out are grunts!"

The voice was shrieking at her, tearing her apart. She felt things giving inside her and a great scream of rage and hatred exploded inside her. It surged up, building, rising. It burst from her, not as a scream, but as a great sob, a terrible moan of helplessness, fury, and anguish, the cry of a wounded animal. She hurled her books at the hated face in front of her and watched them explode in bursts of white pages in the air. Turning to flee from the room she blindly crashed into chairs and desks until, with great wracking sobs, she collapsed against the door, found the knob and fell into the empty hall outside. Still sobbing, she clutched at the handrail as she stumbled down the stairs and ran down the hall toward the exit.

She passed Bernice's open door then found the double doors. She leaned against the push bar and caught her breath. Suddenly Bernice was there.

"What is it, Nancy?" she asked. "What happened?" She put her arm around Nancy's shuddering shoulders.

Nancy calmed slightly and stared out the glass of the door at the gravel outside. "It's Quigley," she began haltingly. "No, it's not just him. It's Barry and this town and my father and Grebs and, and..." She tried to wipe the tears away with the back of her hand. "I just have to get away. I have to get out of here."

"OK, leave then," Bernice said. "But *do* something, Nancy. Don't just run away and hide. Find the strength you need to come back here, to untangle this knot, to make sense out of this place." She waved out the door toward the river and mountains and the town along their edges. "It's all here. All the beauty and ugliness, the hope and helplessness. All the love and hate and joy as well as the suffering. Everything you need is here."

"But why here? It's too hard here," Nancy whispered.

"Because this is where your people are. This is where your roots are, and they're old, strong roots, Nancy, old as mine. When I was a child I went to public school all day, but when I came home I went to Chinese school for two hours. Sometimes I resented not being able to play with the other kids, to be on teams or watch T.V. It was hard, but slowly I realized that I was finding something that mattered more than all the sports or T.V. shows in the world. I was finding my centre; I was beginning to know who I was. I was developing a way of seeing the world with clarity and understanding. And I was finding the power to change it."

She had been talking quietly but quickly. Now she paused. "I'll never live in Chinatown, and I've taken ways from other cultures. Who knows? Maybe I'll even marry a white man or an Indian. But everyone has to know themselves, start from their roots. Everybody had better have an identity."

Nancy shook her head. "I don't know," she said. "It may have worked for you, but that was another place, another time, another people." She sighed deeply. "I just don't know."

Bernice's voice became louder, almost angry. "Do you think your ways are so weak? They sustained your people for ten thousand years. They faced the same problems — fear, loneliness, weakness, uncertainty. Why are you so sure your ways will fail you now? Have you given them a chance?

"Listen," she said fiercely. "Everybody needs an identity — that's Survival Skill Number One — and if you're Indian it damn well better be an Indian identity. You can change it, adjust it to new circumstances, new challenges, but you better start with your strength — who you are."

"But where do I go?" Nancy asked. "What do I do? I don't even know what I'm looking for."

"It's out there, and if you really want it and are willing to look hard, you'll find it."

Nancy paused another moment, her hands clutched around the aluminum push bar. She looked up briefly at Bernice. Then she opened the door and stepped out into the warm spring sun.

VIII.

Nancy lay in bed until noon each day watching the hands on the clock on her bedside table crawl in a slow circle. When she tried to get up, the warmth of the blankets and the softness of the pillow drew her back into easy oblivion.

When she was finally sick of spending hour after hour drifting in and out of sleep, she dragged herself into the kitchen and sat heavily on an old vinyl-covered chair. Moving the twenty feet from her bedroom to the kitchen seemed to drain her, and she sat staring blankly out the small window above the sink.

She had never felt like this. A terrible listlessness seized her and left her limp, empty. She didn't even feel the warmth of the mug of coffee her father pressed into her hands, and was oblivious to the concern written across his face. She spent hours on the back porch looking blankly out over the edge of the bench to the mountains. Nothing registered. The vivid greens of the pines, the patches of grass, and the new leaves of the alders and saskatoons hazed grey and dull, and the dramatic backdrop of the mountains beyond the river was flat and indistinct. The chittering of the birds, the soughing of the wind through the trees, and even the growing warmth of the spring sun went unnoticed as Nancy shivered in the shadows thrown by the porch roof.

Often she cried for no apparent reason. There were no particular thoughts she was aware of; indeed, her whole head seemed clogged with sawdust. She moved and spoke without reflection or awareness. And the tears seemed to spring out of her eyes with astonishing spontaneity. Sometimes she would merely glance at her father bent over his carving, and she would start weeping. Other times she would be rocking in the old rocking chair on the porch and would feel her throat close up and the tears sting her eyes, as great waves of sadness swept through her.

Sometimes a memory of Barry laughing in the bar or the angry face of Quigley would trigger the heaving emotions. Other times she would be Barry on the bridge, hesitating, then leaping off the edge, falling and falling. But often it was a deeper sadness, the sadness over some great, incalculable loss that she could neither define nor comprehend. It welled up inside her like a black wind that rushed through her, leaving her feeling more empty and desolate than she had ever felt before. She was depleted and tired, exhausted beyond normal fatigue.

Her father tried to talk with her, but he was confused by her withdrawal and anguish. For so long Nancy had been the strong one, the one who had counselled, directed, and listened to him. Now she was locked in a terrible silence, and he felt helpless to break it.

The third morning he knocked on her door and entered the bedroom. "Aren't you going to school today?" He felt nervous and awkward, uncertain about what to say or do. He ran his big brown hands through his hair. "Nancy, you've gotta go to school."

Nancy didn't even turn over. "No, Poppa, I don't. I'm not going back there."

"But you can't just quit," he said, his deep flat voice betraying his worry. "You're too close to finishing."

"Yes I can," Nancy murmured. "And you don't know how far away from finishing I really am. Miles away. Centuries away..." Her voice trailed off into muffled sobs as she pressed her face into the pillow.

He looked at the thin body shaking under the covers and he wanted to reach out to her. But his hand hesitated, then halted, and slowly dropped back to his side. "Is it because of Barry? Is that why you're so sad?" he asked softly.

There was a long silence until finally the crying tapered off. "I don't know, Poppa," Nancy answered feebly. "No...yes. I don't know. Barry and you and them and us. I don't know."

Her father stood by the side of the bed, his face twisted in pain and bewilderment. "I...I wish I could do something." He looked helplessly around the room as if he might find the words hidden somewhere. "I don't know what to say."

Nancy remained huddled in her bed, her face buried in the pillow. Finally, defeated, her father turned and went back to his carving.

The house remained almost silent until George came on the fourth day. His truck banged over the rutted drive and lurched to a stop. Nancy, sitting on the back porch, vaguely heard him close the truck door and walk into the kitchen. She heard the low murmuring of conversation between her father and George, then George's heavy footsteps as he walked through the house and onto the porch. The screen door slammed behind him and he sat on the railing in front of her.

"Nancy," he said gently. "What's going on? You haven't been to school for three days. Maria Adams said you had an argument with Quigley and walked out of school. Why didn't you talk to me?"

Nancy felt suddenly moved by the hurt and concern in his voice. She closed her eyes and tears spilled slowly down her cheeks. "I'm sorry," she whispered. It was hard to talk and the words came in gasps. "I didn't talk to anyone except Bernice. I came right home and I haven't felt like going anywhere since." Now her weeping turned to sobs, and she buried her face in her hands, leaning forward in the chair.

He came to her and put his arm around her shivering shoulders. Drawing her close, he held her tenderly until the moans and sobs subsided at last. Finally she raised her wet face and looked at him with red swollen eyes. "I'm sorry, George."

"For what?" he asked quietly.

"For crying and staying in bed. For being scared and angry. For being lonely and lost. For being so afraid."

George rocked her back and forth. "Hey, there's no reason for being sorry for all that. We all feel that way sometime. But listen, Nancy, what are you going to do? You can't stay here forever. You've got to do something. Like going back to school."

Suddenly anger overcame her grief and confusion. She sat back and thrust George away, sending him sprawling against the railing. "Damn you, George. If all you came here for was to act like a truant officer you can leave right now."

George got up, anger flashing in his own eyes. "All you've talked about since I've known you is how you want to get through school and leave this place," he said. "Now here you are, less than three months from finishing, and you're throwing it all away. I can't let you do that."

"And how do you propose to stop me?" Nancy demanded. "Are you going to club me and drag me by the hair up to the school each day? Maybe you can handcuff me to my desk. This is my life and I'll do what I want with it, understand?"

The two glared at each other for a few seconds, then George's eyes softened. "What do you want to do with it then?" he asked.

Nancy's anger cooled and her eyes shifted vacantly away from George's face, over his shoulder, and toward the mountains beyond. "I don't know," she whispered, as the old empty longing again opened up inside her. "I just don't want to end up like Barry."

George reached over and held her hand. "Then don't. But you

67

can't just hibernate here. You have to do something. Don't go back to school now, but you've got to find something to snap you out of this."

Nancy nodded. "OK, George. I will. I'll really think about it and do something."

"Promise?"

She smiled. "Yeah I promise." She leaned over and gave him a hug. "And thanks."

She watched him as he drove back toward the ferry. The night was closing in and she could just make out his hand as he waved from the truck's open window before disappearing into the pines. Once back in the house where her father was drinking coffee, she realized that he hadn't had any alcohol in the three days she'd been home. Now he sat near the crackling warmth of the wood stove and stared absently out the door she'd just entered.

Nancy poured herself a cup of coffee from the enamelled tin pot that simmered on the stove. She studied her father as he sat hunched over his coffee, his great gentle hands folded around the cup as if for warmth. She stepped over to him and hugged his broad shoulders.

"Pop," she said quietly. "I'm sorry I've been moping around here for the last four days. I'm just... I'm just not sure what to do. After Barry's death things stopped making sense. Or they never did make sense and I just began to realize it. Anyway, I feel kind of lost, you know? School has always been meaningless, but now it seems even more ridiculous. I just can't go through that charade right now. So I don't know where to turn, or who to turn to."

Her father looked up at her and smiled sadly. "I'm sorry, too, honey. I'm sorry I don't know how to help."

They looked at each other for a moment. "Maybe I should go away, travel for a while," Nancy continued. "Maybe go to Vancouver and get a job for a while." She said it tentatively, uncertainly.

"Maybe," her father said.

"Or maybe like Bernice said, it's all right here. Maybe I can figure things out without leaving. But I just don't know how."

Her father looked down at his hands on the table. "When my great grandparents were young, things were simpler. Our people learned who they were from the elders and the quests. But now the elders are gone and no one goes on spirit quests anymore."

"What about Grandma Antoine? She still knows about the old

ways."

Her father shrugged. "But she went through residential school too. She never learned the spiritual ways and there was no time for her to go on her quest. The priests didn't give time off for that sort of thing, you know."

Nancy sensed something slipping away. For a minute there had been the beginning of an idea. "But there must be someone who can help, who can teach me." Her voice was tense, almost desperate.

Nancy's father thought silently for several seconds. "There may be some people up at Twenty-six Mile who do sweats, but I don't know." Slowly, he looked up at her. "Then there's old Cecile Schmidt."

Nancy's face fell. Old Mrs. Schmidt lived by herself about a mile down the river from them in a little red house on the edge of a tiny bench. People rarely saw her, and when they did she was generally scowling. Some of the people used to whisper that she was a witch, and when Nancy was young kids used to dare each other to go knock on her door. "I'm not going over there," Nancy could remember squealing. "She might turn me into a raven." Nancy had called her Old Mrs. Schmidt ever since she could remember and though she looked about fifty she never seemed to age. Now, Nancy figured she had to be at least seventy-five.

"Pop," Nancy protested, "I don't want to get mixed up with Old Mrs. Schmidt. She's, she's spooky!"

Her father just smiled. "She's not so bad. It's just that she keeps to herself. She grew up with her grandparents and she only went to residential school for a few years when she was older. I don't know why. Maybe her grandparents hid her or maybe they said they needed her at home. Anyway, she grew up with her grandparents right where she lives now. Then she disappeared for a while. I don't know where she went. Years ago she came back with a new name, but she moved right back into her old house. She's been there ever since. When she came back she spent most of her time with the elders. She knows more about the old ways than anyone else around here."

"Geez, Pop. I don't know." The thought of going to Old Mrs. Schmidt's house brought back a rush of the same fear she remembered having as a child. "Maybe we should just forget the whole idea."

Her father shrugged again. "It's up to you. But if you want to talk

69

with someone about the old ways, I can't think of anyone better than old Cecile."

Nancy stood thoughtfully by the table and sipped her now-cooled coffee. "Pop," she asked finally, "is Old Mrs. Schmidt a witch?"

Her father chuckled. "When we were kids the nuns used to tell us her grandparents were heathens because they didn't go to church. But I never saw Cecile flying around on a broomstick."

"Can she, you know, change people."

"You mean into something else?"

Now it was Nancy's turn to grin. "I know that sounds ridiculous, but that's what the kids used to say."

"I only heard of Coyote doing that," her father replied, his face brightening at the memory of legends learned long ago and almost forgotten.

Nancy paused again. Now her coffee was positively cold. She set it down on the table. "OK. Maybe I'll walk over there tomorrow and pay a visit. You know, just say hello."

Her father got up and walked into his bedroom. Nancy heard him rummaging around in a drawer. Soon he returned with an old bear's tooth strung on a buckskin thong. He slipped it around her neck.

"This was my great-grandfather's. The bear was his guardian spirit and gave this to him on his spirit quest. He wore it and believed it kept away evil. It was especially powerful against witchcraft he said. Later, my father gave it to me when I was a boy, but I never paid much attention to it. Now I'm giving it to you."

"You mean because of Old Mrs. Schmidt?"

Her father smiled sheepishly. "Well, you can't be too careful."

And they both laughed for the first time in days.

IX.

It wasn't until early afternoon that Nancy started for Old Mrs. Schmidt's; somehow there seemed to be a lot of chores to do first. But finally she couldn't find any other reason to put it off, and she began the fifteen minute walk. Before closing the front door she ran her fingers nervously around the thong that hung around her neck. She pulled up the bear's tooth and glanced at it just to make sure it was still there. The two-inch tooth was smooth and reassuring in her fingers. She dropped it back down the front of her blouse and started toward the road.

The warm April sun was melting the snow at the higher levels, and streams splashed noisily down the mountains and under the road. Otherwise the day seemed ominously quiet, and Nancy walked with increasing reluctance. As she rounded the last turn and neared the path that led to Mrs. Schmidt's her step faltered and her heart started pounding. In front of her stood four nearly identical ponderosa pines — two at each side of the path. They were massive, their tapering trunks a deep red. Huge limbs jutted from them, forming an almost perfect arch across the path. She paused at the opening, peering through the branches. But the trail twisted through trees and underbrush and was quickly lost to sight.

Nancy stepped across the thick roots that lay partly above the sandy soil like half-buried snakes. Then she quickly stepped back, shook her head disgustedly, and tried again. But after two steps into the shade under the trees she turned and quickly walked back toward the road.

"This was a stupid idea anyway," Nancy muttered. "What can some weird old lady teach me?"

She reached the road and stopped. Which way should she go? If she went right she'd be back home in a matter of minutes. But then what?

Frozen, she stood there for two full minutes. Finally she turned slowly toward the nearly square opening between the trees. Well, she thought, what do I have to lose? She played nervously with the thong, but this time she passed between the trees without slowing and soon she was in a tunnel of leaves and pine needles that twisted gently downwards. It had been years since she'd been this far, but still she felt the panic she'd known as a child.

71

Finally the underbrush ended and Nancy emerged into a small clearing. The house was small, probably no more than two rooms. Part of it was log, but she couldn't tell whether the other section was framed or also made of logs covered with boards. Long ago perhaps the whole thing had been painted a rusty red; now it had faded into the indefinable hues of a weathered barn. Two narrow windows, one cracked through the centre, faced the trail. A sagging screen door on the left side faced an old wood stove which stood inside an open shed with a slanting shake roof. Strips of cedar roots hung from nails hammered into the posts supporting the roof, and plants Nancy didn't recognize were strung on cords to dry.

The clearing was less than a half acre and the house perched just fifty feet from the edge at the back where the land fell sharply to the river. A well-worn path led to the edge and disappeared over the side. Suddenly, a movement made Nancy jerk her head toward the front of the house. A huge black raven was picking at piles of deer hair near a hide-stretching frame leaning against the only tree on the bench. The bird stopped and looked up, eyeing her curiously.

Nancy walked slowly across the clearing to the door, hesitated, then knocked timidly on the screen door. The weathered door rattled faintly. She waited for a few seconds, then exhaled sharply, feeling an odd mixture of relief and disappointment. "She's not here," she said to herself. But she knocked again, this time harder.

"What do you want?"

Nancy gasped and jumped away from the door, whirling to her left. An old woman with a cedar root basket strapped to her back stood ten feet away, peering at her.

Nancy stared at Old Mrs. Schmidt in astonishment and confusion. Where had she come from? There hadn't been a sound. And what *did* Nancy want anyway?

"Mrs. Schmidt?" Nancy stammered.

"Who are you?"

The blood was pounding in Nancy's temples and her throat seemed to close shut. "Nancy Antoine," she squeaked.

Mrs. Schmidt stared at her with slightly narrowed eyes. The old woman's hair was silver grey and it was tied loosely in the back. "You're Ben Antoine's girl." She said it as a statement. Then she shrugged off the basket and set it down beside her. The cedar root had mellowed to a rich brown, but a jagged design in even darker material was woven around the basket.

"Yes," Nancy said, staring at the basket. "That's a beautiful basket. I didn't know people still really used them."

Mrs. Schmidt grunted. "That's what they were made for."

"But they're so rare. I thought they were all in museums. That one must have taken hundreds of hours to make."

"It was made by my grandmother. Do you know how old it is?"

Nancy shook her head.

"More than sixty years. It's been carrying things for sixty years. A few hundred hours doesn't seem so long when you think about it that way, does it?" She picked up the basket, carried it over to the shed, and dumped the contents out on a rough table. Nancy stared at the tangle of twigs.

"What's that?" she asked.

"Ts'zil." Mrs. Schmidt replied. "Cascara the whites call it."

"Oh." There was a long silence as Mrs. Schmidt's thin fingers deftly sorted the twigs. "Well, what do you use it for?"

"Tea."

"Oh." There was another awkward silence. "Do you drink it for, uh, the taste?"

Mrs. Schmidt turned toward her. "I drink it because I'm constipated. Indians have been drinking it as a laxative for ten thousand years." As she spoke her teeth flashed in perfect white rows. "Is there anything else you'd like to know?"

Nancy felt the tears sting her eyes. Everything was going terribly wrong. She fought an impulse to run back through the trees to the road and leave this wretched woman to her twigs.

"I'm sorry," Nancy managed. "I don't know much about herbs and plants."

Mrs. Schmidt had turned back to her work and only grunted again. She wore a blue blouse, baggy brown pants turned up at the cuff, and a pair of high white tennis shoes. Wisps of grey hair hung over her large ears, and her lined face shone with a deep glow. The skin looked as soft as suede, and Nancy had an impulse to reach out and feel it.

Mrs. Schmidt looked up and pointed to a pail near the stove. "Fill that pail up with water."

"This one?" Nancy picked up the pail. "Is the water in the house? Do you want me to go in the house? Or do you have water out here? Do you want it full or..." she continued nervously.

Mrs. Schmidt looked at her for a long moment. "Use the pump," she said, pointing to a red pump just behind the house.

"Oh, right. Oh." Nancy hurried over to the pump and worked the handle. After several strokes water began gushing out the spigot, but she had forgotten to put the pail underneath and it splashed onto the ground. She hurriedly set the pail down and glanced at Mrs. Schmidt, who seemed preoccupied with starting a fire in the old stove. Nancy went back to the pump handle and filled the pail.

She lugged the water back to the shed as a fire started crackling in the stove. Mrs. Schmidt took an old enamelled dipper and transferred water to a large beat-up pot which she placed on the stove. "Always think before you pump," she muttered.

Nancy was startled. "What?"

"The pump. Always think before you act."

Nancy nodded. She watched in silence as Mrs. Schmidt brought the water to a boil and stuffed the pot full of cascara twigs. She put a lid on, and soon pungent steam was spurting out.

"Why do you have your stove out here?" Nancy asked.

"Gets pretty hot in there in the summer." She gestured at the little house. "Especially with a wood stove fired up."

"But what do you do in the winter?"

Mrs. Schmidt looked at her and shook her head. "I've got another one inside." She smiled tolerantly at Nancy, and again her beautiful white teeth lit up her face.

"Oh."

The old woman turned back to the stove and used an old rag to pull the pot off the stove. She dipped out the tea and poured it in an old white mug that had been hanging over the stove. Then she pulled down another cup and offered it to Nancy. "Want some?"

"Well, uh, no. Not really. I've been pretty, you know, regular." She tittered in embarrassment.

"Suit yourself." Mrs. Schmidt grinned again then raised her left hand to her mouth. Nancy's eyes widened as the old woman spit her teeth into her hand and placed them in a glass on the top of the stove. Then, sipping the strong-smelling tea, she pointed her chin at the dentures.

"I lost mine years ago. False teeth are about the only thing the white man gave us that's worth a damn. I always take them out when I drink tea. Keeps them from getting stained."

Nancy watched in silence as Mrs. Schmidt drank three cups of the cascara brew. "Well, I guess I should be going," the girl said, looking

74

up at the sun as though it was a clock.

Mrs. Schmidt looked at Nancy over the rim of her cup and nodded slowly.

"Uh, maybe..." Nancy took a deep breath. "Maybe I could come again? Maybe tomorrow?"

She looked anxiously at Mrs. Schmidt, fearing derision or outright rejection, desperately hoping for some sign of encouragement.

"I'll be here," Mrs. Schmidt said, still sipping her tea. "And when you come tomorrow, maybe you can tell me what you want." There was a twinkle in her dark eyes.

Nancy nodded eagerly and almost ran through the clearing. Reaching the path which led toward home she paused and looked back to see Mrs. Schmidt standing by the shed and studying her intensely. Nancy had the impulse to wave, but thought better of it and walked briskly back along the trail.

X.

"Pop," Nancy said to her father over coffee the next morning. "I think she kind of likes me, but I don't know how to talk to her. I don't even know what to ask her."

"You mean Cecile?"

"Yeah, Old Mrs. Schmidt. She still scares me to death. How am I supposed to approach her?"

"Well, she is an elder, so treat her with respect."

"But what does that mean? Is there anything I can give her or something?"

Her father thought for a while. "There's tobacco. That was a sacred herb to many tribes, and giving it has become a way of showing respect or honour. I don't know, maybe that would work."

"You think so?" Nancy asked hopefully. "Do you have any?"

Her father looked pained. "I've got one unopened can of Players, but that's my back-up. I'm almost out."

"Come on, Pop. Be a sport. We'll be going into town soon."

He sighed, got up and walked back into his bedroom. He emerged with a new tin of Players, the seal still intact.

Nancy took the tin eagerly as her father pushed it reluctantly across the table. "I hope this does the trick," she ventured.

"Me too," her father replied, ruefully.

"Do I say anything special?"

He shrugged his big shoulders and smiled. "Beats me."

"Well, it's worth a try anyway." She hugged him. "Thanks, Pop."

"Sure. Oh, and if things don't work out, ask her if I can have my tobacco back, OK?"

This time the trip to Mrs. Schmidt's seemed shorter and the entranceway less intimidating. But Nancy still found her steps slowing as she got to the clearing. Her hand hesitated as she raised it to knock on the screen door.

"I'm over here."

Again Nancy jumped in surprise: she hadn't seen the old lady but her voice was nearby. She turned toward the shed where Mrs. Schmidt was sitting on an upturned log, weaving a basket. She never glanced at Nancy as her fingers nimbly worked on the round disk in her lap. Nancy walked over to her and watched silently. Mrs. Schmidt had made a circle about eight inches in diameter. She carefully wrapped thin, pliable strands of cedar root around a core of thin cedar sticks which she'd bunched together. Then she punched a hole in the outside coil and pulled the long strand of cedar through tightly. Each coil was perfectly even, about a quarter of an inch thick, and absolutely symmetrical. Nancy watched in silence as the spiral grew with painstaking slowness.

"Those are cedar roots, right?" Nancy asked. Mrs. Schmidt nodded once. "What's that punch made of?"

"Thigh bone from a deer still works better than anything else."

"How do you prepare the roots?"

"Well, first you have to find the right ones. The best roots grow near the surface along the trunks of old rotting trees. That keeps them straight. Once you get the roots, you have to split them so they're just the right thickness and width." She gestured at a bundle of strands about four feet long hanging from a peg in the shed.

"What are you making?" Nancy asked.

Mrs. Schmidt put down her basket and looked up for the first time. "This is a tray for a teacher." She smiled slightly. "He'll pay me about $80.00. That works out to about fifty cents an hour, but it feels good to do this. Not many of us who know how to do it left, you know. I remember meeting a woman from up north. She made birch baskets. She asked me why we made such complicated baskets that took so long. I told her that my people are mountain people. We live in tough country and need tought baskets." She picked up the disk and looked at it critically. A step-like pattern was imbricated from the centre. "No one in the world makes baskets exactly like we do."

"What's that design?"

"That's the thunder pattern. Made out of chokecherry bark. We have many designs. There's the lightning design on the basket you saw yesterday. And the butterfly and the mountain. Lots of them." Mrs. Schmidt looked at Nancy again. "But you didn't come to talk about baskets."

Nancy felt panic growing in her again. "Here," she blurted out, thrusting the tin of tobacco at Mrs. Schmidt.

The old woman looked at the tin, then looked at Nancy. Her eyes narrowing, she studied the girl for what seemed like minutes. Nancy felt uneasy and awkward. Had she offended this strange woman in some way?

She was just about to withdraw her hand when Mrs. Schmidt slowly reached out and took the tobacco. She placed it on the ground next to her then returned to staring at Nancy. The silence became unbearable, and Nancy found herself fidgeting with the bear's tooth and staring at the ground, doing anything to avoid the sharp scrutiny of those narrowed dark eyes.

"Do you think I'm a medicine woman?" Mrs. Schmidt finally asked, her fingers caressing the polished bone awl in her lap.

Now Nancy hesitated. She bit her lip nervously and kicked at a rock with her toe. "No. I don't know," she stammered. "I guess I'm just coming to you as a teacher."

"A teacher, eh? I thought all the teachers worked over there." Mrs. Schmidt pointed her chin toward the other side of the river. "What do you need with an old woman like me?"

"Oh, they've got teachers," Nancy said bitterly. "But they can't teach me what I need!"

Mrs. Schmidt sat quietly for a few moments. "And what's that?" she asked softly.

The frustration and confusion left her mute. When she did speak the ideas were jumbled and incoherent. "I don't know, but it's not just dangling modifiers and algebra equations. I mean we learn about parts of a fish, but the fish are disappearing. Then there's history while people are dying on the bridge. And they're drinking themselves to death. And the ones who aren't have given up. My father..." her voice trailed off. "Barry jumped off the bridge. I know he did. Now they want to log the valley and we can't stop them. Some Indians even go along with it. This place is a killer and I hate it, I hate it!" As she spoke the fury built inside her, and finally she was spitting out the words and stamping her feet on the ground. Then she felt the tears come with a rush and she threw her hands up to her eyes as the sobs began. Clenching inside to stop them, she felt her shoulders shudder and she gasped for air.

"Stop that," Mrs. Schmidt said sharply.

"I'm trying to," stuttered Nancy, again trying to hold back.

"That's what I want you to stop. If you need to cry, then cry. Why are you ashamed of crying? Are you going to let the pressure build up until you need a psychiatrist? Or are you going to let the pain go? Do you love it so much that you want to hold onto it, that you can't let go?"

Nancy shook her head miserably.

"As Indian children, crying was part of our training. It's good to release your hurts. I remember when I was a kid I used to cry like I'd never be able to stop." She pulled Nancy down to a log next to her. "And my grandmother would hold me, and 'whisst, whisst, whisst,' she patted my head." As she said this Mrs. Schmidt put her arm around Nancy's shoulders, pulled the girl gently to her, and stroked her hair softly. Nancy felt the sobs breaking inside her, and the tears flowed freely down her cheeks. She cried, and as she cried Mrs. Schmidt's voice, soothing and gentle, continued.

"I used to wonder why my grandmother would talk about someone who had died years before. You know she'd be sitting around with my aunt and other friends. They'd be sitting making baskets and one would start the crying: 'Oh, my oldest son. He died so young.' Then she'd start really crying, heartbreaking crying, and the next one would mourn, really feel for the other, and then the whole circle would be crying. Just sitting there sniffling."

"And of course we kids, we loved them, and we'd be playing and we'd look over and, 'Oh, my God, my grandmother's crying,' and I'd look at her, you know, and pretty soon we'd be sniffling too. We didn't know what they were crying about, but just to see them made us cry."

Mrs. Schmidt continued holding Nancy, and slowly the sobs subsided. "My grandmother used to say they meditated on sadness to bring themselves to cry. And once you had that good cry you released everything. You felt better. She did it all her life. Many times I saw her go away, and an hour later she'd come back, red-eyed and a different person. She said that when you were weighted down and couldn't sort out your mind you could go to your mother, the earth, just like a little child goes to its mother and climbs up into her lap and pounds and pulls her hair and scratches. But the mother just holds the baby. She will just rock it and that baby practically pulls her apart. Finally it gets it all out and it feels OK. It gets down and goes to play.

"We can do the same thing. When you feel everything is going wrong for you, go away from people and go out into the bush far away. If there's a rock or stream, go near them. Get down on the ground and pull the grass, pound on the dirt. Take it all out on them. You can dig into that dirt and have a good cry. Just cry. Let it all out. When you feel you can't cry anymore go to the water. Get into that water and wash. You'll feel better. Many times I have done this. And when you're done you listen and you hear the little birds. The squirrel sitting up in a tree just a-scolding you. If you really know how to listen you can hear the wind going through the needles of the trees. You can almost hear the trees whispering at you.

"And that's what it's all about. You begin to look around and see the beautiful little plants. You have to become close to the earth and its strength. This strength comes from the higher power. It's in the rays of the sun, the wind, the rain."

Now Nancy was just sniffling softly. "I can remember that after my grandmother held me and talked with me for a while," Mrs Schmidt continued, "I just relaxed and stopped crying." Nancy sat up and rubbed her red eyes. "And a few minutes later I'd forgotten all about that crying."

Mrs. Schmidt was blurred, but her bright smile burned through Nancy's tears. "Thank you," Nancy whispered.

"Remember this: as young women we were taught to meditate on things that brought on sorrow. You taught yourself to cry. It's just a tiny part of it all. There's much to learn."

"Will you teach me?" Nancy pleaded. "Please?"

The old woman's eyes clouded over. "I don't know. There's so much... And I only know a small portion of it."

"Please, Mrs. Schmidt." The old woman's eyes cleared at the desperation in Nancy's voice. "I feel like you're my last chance."

Mrs. Schmidt grunted. "Nonsense. I'm no saviour. It doesn't help to make things worse than they are. You have lots of choices. By coming here you've made one of them. Don't forget that. You're in charge. Not me, not the school, not your father. I can only be a guide. That's the whole idea of Indian learning. You experience it. It's your responsibility. You learn directly by listening and watching, by going directly to the source of the mysteries. Then the learning is truly yours. In school you learn through someone else and you learn what they tell you. The answers are theirs. In Indian learning you must gain knowledge through experience. You can't learn from me, just through me."

Nancy wasn't sure she fully understood, but she nodded anyway. "But you'll help me then?"

Mrs. Schmidt sighed. "I'll do what I can. Indian learning doesn't start at seventeen. You know that don't you? When an Indian child was born, that child took his or her place in the family and community. It was trained from the start in discipline and responsibility. Even when a girl was tiny, just two or three, a basket was strapped to her waist. She's probably too small to reach the berries, but she can fill that little basket with leaves and dirt. She learns lesson number one. The basket must be filled up. As she gets older the basket gets larger and the training period gets longer. But all the time the parents, aunts, and grandparents are constantly encouraging the child with love, not by saying 'Here's a quarter. Go get a candy bar!' like they do now. Then when the girl got a little older they began to prepare her for the puberty rites. That was the hardest challenge of all.

"Now the girl was entering a new phase of her life. The child had been learning about life since she was so high." Mrs. Schmidt bent over and held her hand a foot above the ground. "Now, instead of the parents putting them through a test, the girls put themselves through that test. How much have I learned? This was called ssqualmach. Sometimes people call it a spirit quest. It was, too, but it was more a quest for spiritual understanding. Very rigorous. And the strength the girl needed to complete it came from her everyday treatment as a child. And from the spirits she speaks with and prays to."

Nancy always felt uncomfortable when she heard elders talk about spirits. It wasn't exactly that she doubted their existence — at least she was sure they had been very real for the old people — but so much had changed. She could hardly believe they were still out there, waiting.

"Mrs. Schmidt," Nancy asked uncertainly, "do you think they're still around?"

Mrs. Schmidt snorted and looked more sharply at Nancy. "Where do you think they went? You think they said, 'There's too many white folks around and the Indians don't care about us anymore. Let's pack our baskets and head for California. It's warmer there, anyway'? You think they got old and died. Just sort of withered away, maybe?"

Nancy managed a wry smile. "Well, no. It's not that. It's just that so much has happened, so many changes. Maybe we can't find them now. Maybe they can't exist for us. To find them maybe you have to be part of the old way, to see the world through their eyes."

Mrs. Schmidt had gone back to weaving the basket. As she spoke, her fingers seemed to weave the words into the coil that slowly grew in her lap. "Nancy, listen to me. When the old people sent the young people on their quests, they used to say, 'When you can understand the jay talking it's time to come home'. Do you know what they

82

meant by that?"

"Well," Nancy ventured, "either they had spent enough time to understand the speech of the animals or they were cracking up. Either way they should head back."

The old woman gave a quick shake of her head. "This is going to take some time," she muttered. "Do you think they went up into the bush for a year, two years, all by themselves just so they could talk with birds? Look, they were up there to get to their core, to tear away the layers that had built up for fifteen or sixteen years. Do you know what you find when you succeed in doing that? You find the spirit of wonder. You come face to face with the Great Mystery, the Creator, the Big Holy or the Great Spirit. Whatever you call it, it's an energy, and it's in you and every object in the world. But this spirit is unseen. Its creation is nature. We can't understand the Great Mystery, but we can see its reflection everywhere. It's in the thunderstorms, the plants, the animals. It's in the way the dawn follows the night, the way the sun moves across the sky, the way the seasons change, the way rain brings life. Both life and death are the expression of this mystery. And when you open yourself up through purification, blessing, and sacrifice, you can hear it. In the thunder, the river, the jay."

Nancy was silent for a long time. A raven flapped into a pine tree at the edge of the clearing and looked down at her. There was only the quiet rustling as Mrs. Schmidt's fingers pulled the split root through the coils. Then she heard the wind in the trees and, distant and indistinct, the faint hum of the river far below them.

Finally she stirred. "Does that mean it's too late then? For me, I mean. Am I too old?"

"Too old? No, no." Mrs. Schmidt stood up and laid the basket on a shelf inside the shed. "Come inside, it's getting late. I'll tell you a story, one I haven't told many people." She picked up the tin of tobacco Nancy had brought and walked toward the house.

Nancy glanced at the sun slowly edging toward the western horizon. It was early evening, and the single pine in the front of the house threw a long shadow like a thick finger across the clearing. She followed Mrs. Schmidt into the little house. The main room, serving both as kitchen and living room, was small, not much larger than Nancy's bedroom, and the walls were squared logs. Through the doorway she could see a room with a bed and an old white dresser decorated with painted flowers. The whole house smelled of wood smoke. Nancy looked more closely around her. Against one wall stood an old chesterfield covered with a brown cloth. Opposite, there was a small table and three kitchen chairs, and a stove was placed at each end of a counter that held a pail of water, a stack of plates, and a few enamelled cups. One stove was electric, but Mrs. Schmidt walked to the wood stove, picked up some kindling, and began making a fire.

"Why don't you use the electric stove?" Nancy asked, sitting on the old couch.

Mrs. Schmidt walked over to the other stove and opened the oven door. Boxes and tins were lined up on the racks. "White couple I got to know gave me this," she said. "But I don't have the right power — it needs two-twenty watts or something — so I never hitched it up. It makes a great cupboard though." Taking a box of tea bags out of the stove she placed one in a pot. Then she set the tea kettle on the wood stove.

"I told you about the way children were raised in the old days, and that was the way my grandparents tried to bring me up right here. They even tried to keep me out of the residential schools. They told the priests they were too old to look after themselves. Ha! Either one would have taken the average priest two falls out of three."

"My father said you went away for a while."

Mrs. Schmidt looked annoyed. "Can I tell this story my own way?"

Nancy gulped. "Sorry, sorry," she stammered.

"Anyway, I was brought up traditionally. We spoke Shuswap — why, I didn't even learn English till I was almost ten — and I bathed in the stream over there" she pointed through the far room "ever since I was four or five."

"Year round?" Nancy asked.

"Year round, every morning. And I used to listen to the stories in the old log houses with dirt floors. I would learn the dances from the elders. If I'd had a few more years, I guess I'd have known them well enough to remember them today, but just at the age I was really getting interested, they came and took me away to residential school. There was some new policy and they wouldn't allow me to stay home. So I was taken across the river and there was that gap again. I lost my Indianness. Later I had to go back and find it, gather all the information again and really concentrate on it. I had to rediscover it, but that was later.

"By the time the residential school was done with me I was completely mixed up. I was ashamed of being Indian. I used to ask the Creator 'Why did you make Indians? We're supposed to be no good. Our religious beliefs are the work of the devil. They are evil.' I used to really believe it. I used to hate myself for being Indian. The only thing I was thankful for was that I wasn't as dark as some."

The kettle was whistling on the stove. Mrs. Schmidt poured it into the pot and picked up a couple of mugs from the counter. She set them on the table.

"But didn't you visit your grandparents?" Nancy asked.

"Oh, sure, every month or so. My grandmother would massage my head and sing to me in Shuswap. But I wasn't listening, I wasn't interested anymore. I wanted to be a beautiful white lady. This cabin was disgusting. I wanted a big house and a white husband. And I found one."

"You did?"

"Have you heard of any Indians named Schmidt?" she asked wryly. "Oh yeah, I went to Seattle and got a job in a glove factory. Piecework. Six cents a glove. You had to nearly kill yourself to eat. The factory was nearly all Indians and immigrants. No unions, no breaks. So when I met Harry Schmidt I thought he was my ticket to heaven."

"But he wasn't?"

Mrs. Schmidt laughed. "You know, in Indian religion there's no hell. There's just balance and imbalance. It took the white man to create hell, and Harry Schmidt was an expert. He may not have been evil, but, boy, was he out of balance. He hated himself, his life, his world. He schemed to make money, drank all that he made, and took all his anger out on me. I landed in the hospital three times before I had enough courage to leave. And then it was only because an Indian community worker convinced me that next time he would kill me. But where was I to go? I was too ashamed to come home, and besides, I still believed in the white man's dream of wealth and happiness." Mrs. Schmidt stood up and found a packet of cigarette papers on the table. She pulled one out, opened the tin of Players, took out a pinch of tobacco, and rolled it expertly. She took a wooden match from a box, struck it underneath the chair, and lit the cigarette, inhaling deeply.

"So I slid from one city to another, and slowly I realized I was going nowhere. One morning I woke up in a cheap skid row hotel room and I knew I was dying. I packed up what little I had, scraped up enough for bus fare back and came home. And thank the Creator," Nancy thought the old woman's voice shook ever so slightly, "my grandmother was still alive, waiting."

Mrs. Schmidt poured the tea and handed a cup to Nancy. Outside, the sky was darkening and streaks of pink splashed against the blue. Mrs. Schmidt sipped her tea.

"When I came back I realized that the elders had something special, a softness, a strength, that I had been looking for. I had spent years wandering around looking for something, and here it was all the time. I had walked the circle and was back where I started. I worked with the elders, talked with them. Slowly I found the strength I had been looking for, that I'd lost. I guess the scars will always be there. I'm still not real trusting. When I meet someone I still have to look at them from all angles."

"But how did you find it," Nancy asked. "What did you do?"

"That's what I'm getting to," Mrs. Schmidt replied. "After several months of training, the elders advised me to go on a widow's spirit quest. This was traditional when a woman's husband died and she returned to her tribe. When she finished it she was fully accepted again."

"But did your husband die?"

The old woman's voice flared in anger. "How do I know what happened to him? He's dead as far as I'm concerned."

"Yes, of course," apologized Nancy. "Could you tell me about the quest?"

"Well, I could, but I'm not going to," Mrs. Schmidt shot back. "I'll tell you the details some other time. But I will tell you about one part. I had been by myself for about four months practicing the discipline my elders had taught me. I was tired, more tired than you can imagine. And one dusk, much like this, I sat on a rock. I just went numb. At first I thought I was sleeping, but I guess I was in a trance. My spirit went out and I saw myself by this lake way up in the mountains. The water was just blue, and there was a loon up there by itself, swimming around. I was sitting there and the moss was so soft. I couldn't hear myself when I was walking. It was so quiet that I heard a little pebble when I threw it in the lake. I knew this was no dream; I was really there. I can remember every little thing. Every little plant around me.

86

"The loon got out of the water and came up to me. All of a sudden it started talking. It told me that if I was ever sad and lonely or if nothing was going right for me I should sing its song, and the loon taught me her song. When I came out of the trance —I don't know how much later —that song just stayed with me and I kept singing it all the time."

The old woman stopped speaking and there was silence for a minute. Twilight filtered through the windows. Then her voice started chanting the song. It welled out of her, high and lilting, and as she sang her delicate hands danced in the air in front of her. Watching her in the dusk, Nancy saw the loon bobbing and swimming on the blue lake.

"Oo hoo oo. Oo ho hoo oo. Hoo hoo. Oh oh ho hee. Oh ho oh ho oh. Ay hey ay. Oh he ah. Oh hoo hoo. Oh hoo oo."

Then there was silence again. It stretched on for seconds, then minutes as darkness covered the windows and seeped into the small room. Mrs. Schmidt's face became indistinct. Finally she broke the quiet. "So you see, Nancy," she whispered. "They're still here."

Nancy stood up slowly and carried her cup to the counter. She touched the old woman's soft hand. "Good night, Mrs. Schmidt."

She opened the door into the gentle spring night and walked calmly along the dark path to the road.

XI.

When Nancy walked into the clearing the next morning, a column of smoke spiraled up into the pale blue sky. It seemed to be coming from behind the cabin, near the far edge of the clearing. Nancy peeked around the side of the house and saw Mrs. Schmidt, pitchfork in hand, poking at a large fire. She was wearing what looked like an old housecoat and her hair was tied in a red scarf.

Nancy walked behind the house and over to the fire. As she got nearer she noticed a low, round hut that seemed to be covered in tarpaulins, and a small stream that widened into a tiny pool beside the hut. Mrs. Schmidt looked up for a moment, then stared back at the fire.

"You're late," she said.

"Late?" Nancy asked. "It's only nine o'clock."

"Sun's been up for hours. You should be too."

"Why? What does it matter what time I get up?"

"Because you learn what you do. If you want to be lazy, get up whenever you feel like it, but if you want to be strong and disciplined, get up to greet the sun, to pray to Day Dawn."

"Who's Day Dawn?"

"The spirit of the day, of the light."

"Oh," said Nancy softly.

They stood silent for a few moments. "The rocks have been ready for an hour."

"Rocks? What rocks?"

"For the sweat. Today we begin your preparation, and we're going to start with a sweat."

Nancy felt fear growing in her stomach. She'd heard about sweats and they scared her. What went on in there? Could she stand the heat?

"Why a sweat, Mrs. Schmidt? Couldn't we just talk for a while?"

Mrs. Schmidt ignored her and stuck the pitchfork into the centre of the glowing mound of coals. Cradling a large rock on the tines she carried it to the low hut where a canvas flap was thrown back from an arched opening. Inside, Mrs. Schmidt placed the stone in a pit dug in the middle of the circular floor. "We'll start out with eight," she said, returning to the fire.

"Why eight?" Nancy asked idly.

Mrs. Schmidt pulled her fork out of the fire and stuck it into the ground. "You sure ask why a lot."

"Do I?" Nancy began. "Well…"

"Sometimes it's important to ask why, but many times it's a way of not listening, of not letting yourself find your own answers. In the white man's classrooms there are always answers, always reasons. They believe that all mystery can be conquered, and that man can control the natural world. They don't listen anymore, they destroy and exploit. To them, truth lies not in the oneness of all things but in separation. To find their answers they try to break everything down into smaller and smaller pieces, to dissect and analyze and to understand with their heads, not their hearts. But that's the problem. You see, the more you try to split up the world, the more you lose sight of the basic truth: that everything is united. A common spirit moves through every object on this planet. It's in us, the animals, the rocks. That is why we thank the animal for giving up his life for us to live, and why, when we take medicine from a tree, when we break a branch or scrape off the bark, we always talk to that tree and ask it to excuse us. We are bound to the forces of the natural world. To understand them we must listen and open our hearts, not try to analyze them with our brains."

"Do you really talk to trees?" Nancy asked.

"They've got a lot more to say than most people these days. Now I hear even the scientists are saying plants communicate. They hitch lie detectors up to them. They tried an experiment. Six men went by two plants, and the sixth one yanked out one of the plants. Then they hitched up the other plant to a lie detector. The first five go by again, there's nothing. Then the sixth goes by and the lie detector goes crazy. The plant is afraid, and it sends out fear signals." She sniffed. "We Indians could have told them that. But no, they had to figure it out with machines."

"But I still don't understand why I shouldn't ask why," Nancy persisted.

"Because a child who cannot listen, who cannot see, who cannot smell because he or she is too busy asking questions is an under-developed child," Mrs. Schmidt said sharply. "In the white man's classroom they think you're stupid if you don't ask why all the time. In the natural classroom you're learning nothing if you do."

Mrs. Schmidt saw the confusion on Nancy's face and sighed. She took Nancy by the shoulder, pushed her around to look across the river, and pointed toward the town. "Over there Nellie Jack is lying in bed. She's the sweetest, most loving woman I've ever known. And in a little house she's wasting away day by day, dying of cancer. Why? A million people starve in Africa while over here people spend hundreds of millions of dollars a year on pet food and billions on rockets and guns. Why? Your friend, a good young man, killed himself. Why? Can you answer me those things?"

Nancy shook her head slowly. Again, Mrs. Schmidt turned her gently around until they were facing the mountains that rose above them. "And over here, why do the otters play in the river? Why do the little red squirrels chatter and scold? Why are the stems of the sunflowers round and fuzzy? Why does the loon cry over the lake in the evening? Why, when we stand on a mountain ridge and look over a deep wooded valley do we feel awed and quiet? Can you answer me these things?"

Nancy shook her head again.

"Much knowledge can be gained from asking why. But the knowledge and understanding you are seeking here cannot come through me. For there may be no answers or my answers may be wrong. The wisdom you're seeking must be learned directly. You must open yourself, make yourself ready, then go to the mysteries to find your own answers."

She plunged her pitchfork back into the coals. "As for the eight stones," she shrugged, "why are there four directions? Four seasons? This ceremony is done in multiples of four. We sweat four times, add new rocks by fours. That is the way it is done. This is a grandmother sweat," she continued. "The door faces east towards the rising sun."

She continued forking the large stones into the sweat lodge until Nancy could see them glowing in the dark interior.

"I, I've never been in a sweat before," Nancy began. "What do I do."

"For starters, get out of those clothes."

Nancy unbuttoned her shirt and slipped off her runners and jeans. She piled them near the lodge and stood naked. The morning air was still cold, and she hugged herself against the chill. Mrs. Schmidt undid her robe and hung it on a nail driven into a fir tree.

"Before you get in, I want you to think about all your ancestors and elders who have passed along to the spirit world. I want you to ask them to come along into the sweat and guide and guard you. Invite them in to help you find strength."

91

Nancy tried, but it felt strange, awkward. She snickered in embarrassment.

"Listen to me, Nancy," Mrs. Schmidt said sternly. "You are too taken with yourself. You are exaggerated. You have not come here today by accident. These ceremonies have helped two hundred generations of your people to find strength and knowledge. The knowledge and teachings of your ancestors are here today if you will open yourself to them. You must regain a sense of balance. Think about your ancestors and ask them now for guidance."

Nancy closed her eyes. Her mind turned towards her grandparents. Then, slowly, like a heavy mist being lifted, she imagined her other ancestors, living here, in this place. She saw them in an immense line that stretched back for ten thousand years. She was at the head of their blood line, and looking back, saw them smiling at her. "All my relations," she murmured.

"Good," said Mrs. Schmidt. "That's good. Now step into the lodge."

Still pondering the vision, Nancy dropped onto her hands and knees and crawled into the lodge. The ground was covered with fresh fir boughs, and the bent saplings that supported the roof arched barely above her head. She crawled to the side of the lodge and sat still. Then Mrs. Schmidt crawled in, pulling a bucket of water with her, and yanked the flap closed over the door. The heated rocks gave off a dull glow, but otherwise the little lodge was utterly dark. Silently Mrs. Schmidt dropped small fir branches onto each rock, and they burned instantly in a wisp of pungent smoke. She then began a slow wavering chant in Shuswap. As the song filled the lodge Nancy sat silently, listening. The fir needles poked into her bare legs, but the heat of the rocks felt good. This isn't so bad, she thought.

At last Mrs. Schmidt stopped. "I've purified the rocks and prayed for strength and guidance." She took a ladle from the pail and poured water on the stones. Nancy could just make out Mrs. Schmidt's hand in the dark, but her voice seemed separated from her body.

Suddenly the steam hit Nancy like a suffocating blistering-hot blanket. She gasped and desperately tried to breathe, but the heat made it almost impossible, and what air she did manage to gulp in was thick and choking. Quickly, she began to panic as she felt herself smothering.

"If you have trouble breathing," Mrs. Schmidt's voice was calm and reassuring, "put your head down near the ground." Nancy immediately pitched forward, thrusting her mouth into the boughs. Sure enough, the air seemed thinner, breathable and almost cool. "It will become less difficult as the steam cools and you get more used to it," Mrs. Schmidt continued. Nancy looked toward the voice. Now that her eyes had become accustomed to the dark, she could just barely see the old lady's slim figure sitting straight and unconcerned.

She began to speak in the same unhurried tone. "I said earlier that we were going to begin your preparation for your ssqualmach."

"Ssqualmach? Didn't you say that was a spirit quest?" Nancy gulped. She managed to sit up, and her heart was pounding.

"Yes, or puberty rite. Whatever. It's a quest for spiritual understanding, for strength, discipline, and responsibility."

"Listen," stammered Nancy, "this is moving pretty fast. I don't think I'm ready yet. I just wanted some advice, you know..."

"Why did you come to me?"

Nancy paused, staring ahead in the steamy gloom. "I don't really know," she finally said. "Maybe I wanted you to heal me."

"I can't heal you, Nancy. I've told you that you can only learn some things from me. The rest you have to do on your own, and that takes sacrifice and discipline. You have to want it. All I can do is help prepare you."

"Can't you just give me some counselling?"

Mrs. Schmidt gave a short laugh. "You've come to me for strength, not weakness. The way white people do it now they go to psychiatrists to sort out their minds. But even after they come from the office they're still weak. You can go to a psychiatrist many times, and if you don't have the willpower, the balance, the self-knowledge, you will not find strength. Through the sweats, fastings, running, prayer, bathing, and the quest you can find the strength and discipline to transform youself, but you have to really want it. No one, no shaman, no psychiatrist, can do it for you." Mrs. Schmidt paused. "Do you want to go ahead with it?"

Nancy's eyes were fixed on the glowing rocks before her. Like a single unblinking eye they stared back. And all around her the darkness spread forever. "Yes," she said quietly.

Mrs. Schmidt threw back the tarp over the entrance, and Nancy was almost startled to see daylight through the opening. "Come on," Mrs. Schmidt said. "We'll bathe now."

Nancy stepped out of the lodge into the mild morning, noticing how soothing the cool air was on her skin. She followed Mrs. Schmidt around the back of the lodge to the creek that ran through the edge of the trees. A line of rocks had been piled up downstream, backing the river into a pool about eight feet across. Mrs. Schmidt strode unhesitatingly into the water and was soon submerged up to her neck, rubbing herself briskly.

Nancy followed, but she recoiled as the icy water sent a jolt up her leg. Coming directly off the snow from the mountains above them, Nancy guessed the water couldn't have been more than a few degrees above freezing. Grimacing, she forced herself into the clear pool until it was swirling around her waist. Trying to appear nonchalant, she plunged forward, feeling as though she'd been kicked in the chest. The air wheezed out of her lungs, and her whole body seemed paralyzed. After a struggle and a moment of near-panic, she regained her feet, wide-eyed, gasping for breath, and sputtering.

Mrs. Schmidt kneeled in the water and chuckled. "It's a little startling the first time, eh? But it gets easier. I started doing this when I was a tiny child. Learned to do it each morning, winter or summer. After a while I didn't need my grandmother to coax me. I did it myself. I was learning discipline."

Nancy was too cold to speak. Her lower body felt frozen.

"The water is a symbol of strength and cleansing. Water is powerful. It can move boulders. It can move a mountainside, and yet it is so gentle. Later you'll learn to scrub yourself with fir boughs. Now let's return to the lodge."

Nancy splashed hurriedly from the biting water and fled thankfully back to the warmth of the hut. She sat huddled in the lodge while Mrs. Schmidt forked in four more rocks. "This will be hot," Mrs. Schmidt warned.

Good, Nancy thought, still shivering.

Mrs. Schmidt again burned the tip of a fir bough on each rock. "This time," she said as the needles burst into flame, "I want you to think about cleansing yourself. Not just your body, but your mind and your soul as well. You can't just come in here for the fun of it."

Not much chance of that, Nancy thought, beginning to feel the uncomfortable heat again.

"Yes, the sweat is hot, and the water is cold, but that is part of gaining inner strength. You must really want it. Remember, we are always struggling for strength within ourselves. Without that strength we are nobody, eh? Anything that comes around sways us. It's always inner power we're praying for, that you'll do the right things in life. Now first, I want you to think of cleanliness of body and spirit. Clean your mind of clutter and chatter. Make yourself blank and empty. Purify yourself."

As she said this she splashed water over the rocks and heat billowed up in a scalding cloud. Nancy dropped again to the fragrant branches, but this time it didn't take quite as long to be able to sit upright. She concentrated on letting the heat burn the thoughts from her mind. She closed her eyes, and there was just the heat and the darkness and the soft chant. The sweat ran in streams down her face and arms and between her breasts. She felt her pores opening and the live steam scouring her while she meditated on one thought: I want my body, my mind, my soul to be purified. The heat, the chant, and the darkness enveloped her like comforting arms. And that was all.

"Now," came Mrs. Schmidt's soft voice, as if from a great distance, "pray for strength. Ask the Creator and your ancestors to help you find the strength to walk the right road. And ask for blessing on your family, your people, all people, for when they are strong, you are strong."

It seemed awkward, unfamiliar, to ask for help and guidance. Who or what was she asking? Then she saw again the long line of her ancestors, and as she studied their faces she saw the strength in them. She knew they would help her. Strength, she thought, please help me find strength. Please help. The request became a plea, and she felt herself wanting with all her heart the strength of those ancestors, their calm, their knowledge, their balance. It filled her up and choked her until she felt tears mingling with the sweat.

Suddenly the entrance cover was thrown back and light and cool air filtered into the lodge. Nancy shook herself, startled, and followed Mrs. Schmidt silently to the pool. This time the cold water made her skin feel as though it was on fire, and the shock again drove her breath away. But she lowered herself into the pool without protest.

The third sweat began with no new stones. "You are a young girl," Mrs. Schmidt said, "and you are not used to this. As you go along you will increase the stones to sixteen, twenty-four, and thirty-two as your body adjusts. Each rock is a gift from your ancestors that you receive gratefully."

95

She lowered the flap over the entrance and once again it was utterly dark except for the glow of the stones. Mrs. Schmidt poured water over them, and there was the heat, the darkness, and the old woman's soft voice.

"I want to tell you a story about strength, about the strength of our ancestors; strength that is available to you. It is the story of Chuchupauwt, which means Trail of Blood. He was a Kinbasket, and this happened not that long ago. He was still alive when my grandmother was a girl.

"This day he was hunting high up on the plateaus and he came across a grizzly bear. He tried to kill the bear, but he only wounded it. The grizzly bear attacked him. In those days the hunters always carried a big, long piece of bone which was attached to a piece of leather tied to the wrist. It was very sharp at both ends. If you shot a bear and it attacked you, right away you grabbed for that, and when the animal opened its mouth you shoved it in with one end up and the other down, and it left the mouth wide open. Well, that's what saved Chuchupauwt.

"He was mauled something terrible, but he finally killed that bear with his knife. You always either gave your life or killed the animal. This was pride. You fought until you or the animal dropped. Chuchupauwt was bleeding all over his body and he lay almost unconscious on the ground, but he began to sing his song, and his spiritual strength returned."

She paused and ladled more water over the rocks. There was the sound of the water flashing into steam.

"So he started back down the mountain, but halfway down he lost so much blood he started crawling, and he crawled right back down to the river where the other people were camped. He told them what had happened and he passed out. Of course the old women started bringing in medicine, different kinds of herbs, and caring for his wounds. The men went up and all they saw was this trail of blood, and they followed it right up to where the grizzly bear was.

"After that man recovered, he was scarred and disfigured, but he was much honoured among his people. They had a naming ceremony, and all the elders sat in a circle with a medicine man in the middle. Each elder stood up and said what they thought of this man's bravery and strength. They praised him, then they wet his head and he was given his new name — Chuchupauwt, Trail of Blood."

When Nancy entered the pool for the third time, she was conscious of a deep weariness that even the ice-cold water could not wash away. When she returned to the sweat lodge for the last time she sat quietly, a great sense of emptiness inside her. Mrs. Schmidt brought in four more stones from the fire and purified them. She closed the flap and all was dark once again. This time she put two, three, four ladles of water on the sixteen rocks, and the burst of live steam rocked Nancy backwards. This was the hottest yet, and she struggled to breathe.

"Now," Mrs. Schmidt said through the steam, "I want you to speak your requests aloud. I want you to name your emptiness, call out for power and strength. Speak your blessings." Then she began to chant softly.

Nancy opened her lips to speak, but the thick steam seemed to clog her mouth. The words came slowly at first, and they fell dully on the thick air.

"I ask the Creator for strength," she began haltingly. "I pray for the strength to, to do the right things. Not to be easily taken in." Now the words were coming more easily, and there was just her and her requests, crystalized ideas, in a great sweltering darkness. "Help me to find the strength to listen with all my heart. To find balance again in my life."

She paused and the words swam upward in a wave of emotion. "And help me not to be afraid. Please," she sobbed. "Stop the fear. Help me, HELP ME!" She heard a long wail quavering in the darkness. It was a cry of loneliness and pleading, of fear and hope and pain. It went on and on and filled the small lodge, blending with the steam and the blackness and filling Nancy's senses until she was numb. As the wail tapered off, she thought it had come from Mrs. Schmidt, but Nancy could make out Mrs. Schmidt sitting calmly and quietly, leaning slightly toward the glow of the rocks.

Mrs. Schmidt's mouth wasn't open. It was her own mouth that was stretched wide. The astonishing cry had come from her! She closed her eyes, and the sobs lurched from her until they too finally subsided in silence. Mrs. Schmidt ladled more water on the stones.

"Go ahead," she said, "who else are you praying for?"

The steam seemed to pull the words from her. "And stop the pain and fear of my father, my people. Help all people struggling with their fears. Help those like Barry who are dying from their fears and shame." She saw Barry's face, his sensitive brown eyes alive in the dark, and again the tears came.

"And do you want peace for just your own people?" Mrs. Schmidt said at last.

"Bless all people, and help us all find peace in ourselves so that we can be at peace with each other," she finished.

Mrs. Schmidt's voice rose momentarily in a Shuswap prayer. Then she splashed the rest of the bucket of water on the stones, and a great wave of heat covered Nancy again. Again she was drenched in sweat and felt totally emptied. She closed her eyes and let the steam swirl around her bare shoulders, conscious only of a great hollowness within her. The flap was thrown back and she followed Mrs. Schmidt to the pool.

Afterwards, they sat silently on the grass in the warm sun. Nancy breathed deeply, and the air seemed thin and cool. She lay back, staring up at the sky above her. She felt quiet, exhausted, peaceful. No thoughts flitted through her mind.

Finally Mrs. Schmidt spoke. "You have learned much today, but you have much more to learn if you are to be ready for your spirit quest."

Nancy was still only half listening. "How long are spirit quests?"

"Four months."

Nancy sat up abruptly. "Four months?" she exclaimed. "I can't take four months off now!"

Mrs. Schmidt shook her head. "Everybody's in such a hurry these days. In the old times young women and men would go alone for a year or even longer." She sighed. "What else do you have to do?"

"I have to go back to school. Not necessarily to graduate, but there are a lot of loose ends there. You said that sometimes it's important to ask why. Well, there are lots of people over there who need to be asked. We have to think about what they call learning. And I've been as bad as anybody. I sat back and accepted it all, too. Somebody's got to ask some questions."

Mrs. Schmidt shrugged. "Well, how long do you have?"

Nancy did some figuring in her head. It was now mid-April. If she was to get back for any classes at all she didn't have much time. "I don't know. Maybe five or six weeks."

Mrs. Schmidt sighed again. "Well, it will just have to do. We can begin preparing you immediately and in one or two weeks you should be," she eyed Nancy critically, "more or less ready. Do you think you're fit for a month's retreat?"

Suddenly Nancy wasn't afraid anymore. She smiled. "I don't know. I guess we'll find out."

Then Mrs. Schmidt beamed. "Well, it'll be a start."

"Yes," whispered Nancy. "A start. That's what it will be."

XII.

The sky grew pink in the east, glowing so that the mountains stood out in dark relief. Blackness remained in the west, with the brightest stars still suspended above the shadows of the narrow valley. Nancy sat outside her simple tent — really just a tarpaulin pegged down over a rope tied between two fir trees — and looked around the clearing that had become so familiar. Taking out her knife she cut a notch in the branch stuck in the rocks next to her and counted them all once more to be sure. Thirty. This was her last morning.

She sat naked, oblivious to the early morning chill, and put her fingers in the smudge she'd made by burning cedar boughs. Carefully she dabbed the black soot on her forehead. As she did so, the prayers came easily and simply. "Give me strength that I will be able to think clearly." She brushed the smudge over her ears, eyes, and mouth, saying, "Purify my ears that I will only hear what is good, my eyes so that I will see good, and my mouth so that I will speak good." She drew her fingers over her breast, saying, "Fill my heart with love. Take all evil out of my heart." She continued over her legs and body, begging for strength.

She sat quietly then. Still, like the trees around her. She watched as the pink hue expanded slowly across the eastern sky. Only the low rush of the stream running through the rocks ten feet to her left broke the silence. Not even the birds had awakened yet. She stood up, taking fir boughs from a pile next to her tent, and walked toward the small river. Reaching it, she sat down on a flat stone near the pool in the clearing and stared across the dark surface. It was calm and smooth, moving slowly until it finally spilled by several enormous boulders that backed up the stream into this perfect circle.

Taking a fir bough, she rubbed her body, asking the Dawn that each part of her body would be strong and free of pain and disease. She did this four times, leaving needles clinging to her skin. Then she stepped off the rock into the water. She could feel the strength of the mountains, of the glaciers that fed the stream, in the sharpness of the water. She dove cleanly, gliding upstream, feeling the needles floating away, asking the river to wash away all evil as it was washing away the needles, asking it to cleanse her mind as well as her body.

Then she sat in the shallow water on the smooth sand and watched as the sky turned a light blue. She scrubbed herself with fir boughs and prayed to the Day Dawn, begging for strength, for knowledge. As the early morning sun peeked above the eastern edge of the valley and glistened on her wet hair and shoulders, she felt the power of the water gently surging by her, and its strength filled her.

Pulling herself from the pool, she returned to her camp and started the fire that would heat the rocks for her sweat. With a new sense of wonder she watched and listened as the clearing came alive. Brown dippers began dancing from rock to rock in the river, darting into the pools to emerge far upstream. Chickadees chittered in the firs above her. Somewhere a red squirrel began its endless scolding. The growing light revealed the small glade, surrounded on all sides by rocks and the great trunks of grandfather fir. At first it had all seemed alien and lonely, but now it was soft and alive.

The first days had been the hardest. Mrs. Schmidt had brought her here and helped her set up the tent and build a small sweat house. Despite the training she'd already received from the old woman, Nancy dreaded her leaving and tried to find ways of making her stay. Finally she clutched her by the arm, trembling.

"I don't think I can do it, Mrs. Schmidt. I'm scared. I really am."

Mrs. Schmidt held her and spoke soothingly. "What are you afraid of? The animals do not dislike you. Talk to them. Talk to the river and the trees. They are your sisters and brothers, your friends."

Nancy looked around, but found little comfort in the tall silent trees and the river droning by. She felt panic seizing her, shaking her.

"It's not just that, them, I'm afraid of," she gasped. "It's me. I'm afraid of me. I don't want to be alone for thirty days. What will happen? Maybe I'll crack up or find out that I'm evil."

Mrs. Schmidt shrugged. "No one is all evil or all good. We all have both. Was Coyote all good? No. He could be a trickster, a liar, and a cheat. You will find evil, but you will find good too. And more importantly you will find balance."

Nancy tried to control her trembling. "Are you sure I can make it? Maybe we haven't prepared enough."

Mrs. Schmidt shrugged again. "We have done what we could in the time we had. You have purified yourself in the sweat and you have already begun your fast." Nancy became aware of her shrunken stomach. For four days she had had nothing but broth and water. For four more days she could have nothing but water.

"Remember," Mrs. Schmidt continued, "you have come here with a desire. You know what you want. What you are doing here is very hard. You are stripping away your false self, your false image. You are going to get down to your very core. When you break down the body, that's when the mind opens."

Then she pulled Nancy to her, hugged her, and stroked her hair for a moment. At last she turned to go. "I will leave food for you every fourth day," she said. She looked long and hard at Nancy. "You are stronger than you think. You will find this out for yourself."

Then she was gone, scrambling down the narrow trail between the boulders, and Nancy was more alone than she'd ever been in her life.

The first night she'd been instructed not to sleep in the camp but to wander in the hills above the sandy glade. As the sky darkened she walked slowly and hesitantly up the trail that ran by the small river. The shadows under the trees deepened, blotting out even the meager light of the thin moon. She stumbled along the rocky trail, terrified of leaving it and becoming lost. What was she doing here?

She had climbed high up the western side of the valley when she finally stopped. The trail swerved right underneath a sheer rock face that was undercut, forming a shallow cave. She stood between the rock and the river, alone, hungry, cold, exhausted, and scared. At first she just cried, but soon the cry became a scream of terror and loneliness that was lost in the noise of the river. She screamed and sobbed until she collapsed; then she crawled into the cave and lay face down, smelling the moss and dry grass.

The cold dawn shook her awake. Startled, she sat up and looked around. The weak sunlight was gleaming over the eastern lip of the valley and filtering through the trees. She looked above her on the rock. A foot above her head a figure of a man had been painted in red paint, under two lines. Next to the man was a bird, possibly a raven. Nancy stared at them, trying to fathom some meaning, wondering if they'd been painted by another young woman on her spirit quest, desperately hoping that some message, written just for her five hundred years before, would come clear. But there was nothing. The man remained standing silently under what may have been a rainbow, and the raven watched.

Somehow the paintings soothed her. Others had been here before her. Others had survived this. She stood up and slowly made her way back down the trail, feeling not quite so alone.

It took her almost two hours to get to the camp. The sandy clearing looked inviting, and she slumped to the ground, exhausted.

She longed for a sweat to drive the chill from her and to wash away the fatigue and grime, but she couldn't bathe for the four days of her fast. Instead, she searched the rocks until she found a wild rose bush. She broke off a long twig and carried it to the river, where she drank deeply, feeling her empty stomach cramp. Then she bent the rose branch into a loop and forced it down her throat as Mrs. Schmidt had instructed her. "Hweyentshnt" she had called it. Vomiting. "Throw all that water up," she'd said. "Get all the ugly things out of your stomach."

Nancy gagged. She thrust the twig deeper, and the water poured from her. Her stomach heaved until there was nothing left. She felt utterly spent and empty. Tears ran down from her eyes. In a near daze, she recalled her next instructions. She was to run. She had to run to a destination and back twice. She decided to run to the rock painting. The climb was grueling and her legs felt weak and weary. She had to catch herself against a tree, but she stumbled on to the rock. Then she retraced her steps. But she couldn't do it again. She collapsed on the warm sand and slept.

The rest of the day was spent praying, chanting, and singing with the beat of the small drum Mrs. Schmidt had left for her. "The drum is the symbol of your heartbeat," she'd said. "Listen to it. Sing with it."

As the sun began to set, Nancy waded across the river to the far side. She walked until she found a steep, fairly even slope. It rose rapidly through thin firs and ended in a shale slide that fell sharply from a peak towering above. She waited until the shadow of the western edge of the valley reached the bottom of the slope as the sun set. The shadow moved quickly up through the firs, and Nancy sprinted to keep up. But it was far too fast. Halfway up she was stumbling on wobbly legs, gasping for air, clawing upward after the disappearing shadow as the night covered the valley.

The next three days became a blur of running, hunger, vomiting, exhaustion, tears, and terrible loneliness. The smell of the fir boughs she placed on the floor of her tent mingled with her perspiration in the cold nights and mornings. She remembered begging Mrs. Schmidt to come get her, not to make her do this. And she thought about leaving, just walking down the trail and forgetting all the pain.

But she stayed, and when the fourth day ended and she meditated after her run, there was a curious peacefulness. She had done what Mrs. Schmidt had told her. She had deprived her body of food, comfort, warmth. And her mind seemed clearer now, like a muddy pool that had started to settle. There was less chatter in her head. More silence. Her thoughts had dropped away so slowly she hadn't been aware of it, but now there was clarity, openess.

The next morning she had walked down the path for the first time, her pack on her back. Several miles below her camp the small stream she was following joined the Ts'elht river that came rushing down from high in the mountains. The Ts'elht in turn flowed into the Kwalatkwa. Where the small stream met the Ts'elht, the trail also joined a larger trail. There Mrs. Schmidt had left food. Nancy looked at it wonderingly. It had been eight days since she'd eaten anything solid and four since she'd eaten at all. In the last few days her hunger had seemed less important, but now her stomach rumbled as if sighing at a fond memory. She picked up the bread, cheese, dried fruit, and salmon and put it into her pack. Then she climbed the steep trail back to the camp, barely able to keep from dashing, clothes and all, into the pool.

Now the pattern changed. She was in the pool each day before daybreak, timidly at first but becoming less aware of the cold water each day. Then she ran to her rock, and soon she could manage two trips as her legs and lungs strengthened. In the afternoon she performed the sweat ceremony, prayed and chanted, and sang to the drum. At sunset she raced the shadow up the mountainside, and each day she ran farther and came closer to catching the swift, dark line. Then she bathed again at dusk, rubbing herself with fir branches and praying.

The days became weeks. Nancy watched the moon disappear, then re-emerge to grow larger and brighter. She watched the stars wheel in the night sky. She saw the dark shapes of trout dart in her pool, and she heard the grandfather trees creak at night in the soft winds. She watched as saskatoon and wild rose leaves unfolded, and she picked wild asparagus that rose like spikes on open hillsides and fiddleheads that unfurled under the trees. She was quiet now, and her thoughts were as clear and uncluttered as the pool.

She sat in the growing warmth of the sun, and it felt good. She sat in the silent chill of the evenings and early mornings, and it felt good too. She didn't think about strength anymore, though she continued to pray for it. There was knowledge growing, and a sense of great peace, of balance and centredness, but there was something more that was harder to define. It was awe of the sunsets, and astonishment at the tiny forests of moss. It was wonder at the stars vibrating in the sky. It was feeling the life throb through the trunks of giant firs. It was joy at watching the squirrels leap in great arcs from tree to tree. It was hearing the water gabble through the rocks and knowing that there was nothing more important to listen to. And as conversations became memories, it was most of all knowing that she was not apart from all this, this Great Mystery. She cried, but this time it was for the rush of love and union she felt.

Now there was one day to go. Last night she had beat the shadow to the top of the slope for the first time. Today she would run to the rock paintings for the last time, and she would do it without stumbling or gasping for breath. She looked down at herself. The fire danced over her wet skin and she saw a new tautness that had never been there before. She was lithe and strong and beautiful. She knew she had changed, she could see it, but how much? Had she changed as much inside?

Suddenly a large raven swooped into the clearing and perched on a rock six feet away from Nancy. It eyed her carefully, cocking its head from side to side. It looked familiar to Nancy, and she stared back, fascinated by the big black bird. Then it looked at her and opened its beak. For a moment, one fleeting instant, Nancy thought it was speaking to her. But it fluttered its wings, cawed loudly once, and leapt back into the trees.

The next morning Nancy carefully packed her sleeping bag, tent, and equipment after bathing. She stopped by the edge of the clearing and looked back. The ribs of the sweat lodge, stripped of its tarpaulin skin, blended into the bushes. You'd hardly think I'd been here, she thought. The great trees rose on all sides and the river chattered. Come back, it seemed to say. We still have much to teach you.

Nancy turned and walked the two miles to the trail junction. She saw Mrs. Schmidt, a green bandana tied around her head, sitting quietly looking out on the rivers. She turned as Nancy approached and smiled. It was a deep smile of love and respect and welcome. They hugged each other briefly then stood back. They were both smiling now, looking at each other with shining brown eyes. Finally they turned and walked together down the main trail.

XIII.

It had seemed strange at first to be with people again, and she was grateful that her first contact had been with Mrs. Schmidt. When she had first tried to talk, the words seemed awkward and the muscles in her jaws didn't seem to work right. But Mrs. Schmidt said little, and what she did say was soft and soothing. Slowly Nancy's stories came out, but Mrs. Schmidt seemed curiously uninterested.

"I'm proud of you, Nancy," she had said. "Not many young people — or old people for that matter — would have done what you've done. But the experiences are yours, not mine. You do not need my approval or certification. If you wish to share your experiences, I would like to hear. But if you don't, it's all the same. They are part of you now."

Going home was harder, but her father, too, seemed to respect her privacy. He hugged her when she came through the door, and they sat on the back porch and talked late into the evening. But he did not pry, and accepted the silences between her words.

Her first real shock was her trip into town. The activity seemed frenetic and the noise was deafening. When she went into the cafe, friends smiled and asked her where she'd been.

"I've been studying," she began. "With an elder."

A few nodded and raised their eyebrows, but soon the conversation drifted back to dances and summer plans, and Nancy saw no reason to elaborate. Besides, she found she couldn't stay there very long. The voices seemed loud and sharp and what they talked about didn't much interest her. And the din was absolutely painful. Screeching guitars and unintelligible lyrics blared over the cheap speakers, mixing with the chattering and buzzing of the video games, the hooting and cursing of the players, and the general babble of the people sitting at the tables. How had she never noticed the deafening clamor of the place?

But this was nothing compared to what she would face going back to school. She dreaded it. She thought about just staying on her side of the river and forgetting about the place. But she knew she couldn't. She had to go back. She wasn't entirely sure why, but there was a sense of incompleteness, a struggle that remained unfinished. As she walked up the road that curved to the school, only three days after climbing down from her camp, for some reason she thought about Chuchupawt and his fight with the grizzly. She found herself wishing for a sharp stick to jam into toothy jaws.

She walked through the double doors and stood still. Doughnut was furiously typing, glowering over her glasses at students who interrupted her. Nancy leaned against a bulletin board and watched the students swirl into the lobby and drift down the halls. Above her in big red letters was "DON'T BE A FOOL—STAY IN SCHOOL." Then in smaller letters, "School prepares you for the Future". Nancy recalled that the words, somewhat faded, had been there since the fall. Now she noticed a tiny message someone had lettered in a blue marker below them. "Yeah," it read. "By doing exactly what you are told in school, you are preparing to do exactly what you're told as an adult."

Nancy snickered. She wondered how long that had been up there. Obviously, the staff didn't pay much attention to the bulletin board. If a teacher had seen that it would have been stripped down immediately.

Students spotted her and smiled. Some came over to welcome her back, and some asked where she'd been, but there was little fuss. She had been gone. Now she was back. That was all.

She stepped into the stream and was pulled down the hall to her English class. She walked in and sat at the back. At the front, behind his desk, sat the teacher, Mr. Donaldson. He was a nervous little man who always wore a thin brown tie and the same worn-out green tweed sport coat. As the students shuffled in he appeared to be absorbed in the papers and books that were stacked around him like a barricade. The bell rang shrilly and he finally looked up. His eyes swept by Nancy, then swivelled back suddenly.

"Nancy, I, uh, didn't expect to see you anymore."

Nancy sat silent in her seat.

"Have you, uh, checked in at the office?"

"No," Nancy replied. "I haven't had a chance yet."

"Oh, I see," Mr. Donaldson said. He sat with his pencil poised, obviously unsure of what to do. "Well, I'll just put you down as present on the attendance sheet."

"That seems like a good idea," Nancy agreed.

"What? Uh, yes. Yes."

The class was quiet as Mr. Donaldson checked the boxes by each name in the large blue book spread across his desk. At last he stood up.

"Well, yesterday we reviewed adjective and adverb phrases, and today we're going to move into verbals and verbal phrases. So, we'll get right into it. Please turn to page 387 in your book." Nancy pulled out her book and glanced at the cover: *Learning Effective English.* Someone had carefully lettered a perfect "D" in front of Effective.

"As you know, a prepositional phrase is called a prepositional phrase because it begins with a preposition. Well verbal phrases are so called because they contain a verbal. Now verbals are words that contain some of the characteristics of two parts of speech. They have some of the traits of a verb. They show action and they may take an object. Verbals, however, are not used as verbs in a sentence. Sometimes they act as..." he paused and looked down at the book in front of him. "Yes, sometimes they act as nouns, adjectives, or adverbs. Now the three verbals are participles, gerunds, and infinitives. Participles act as verbal adjectives, gerunds as verbal nouns, and infinitives can work as verbal adjectives, verbal nouns, or verbal adverbs. Now, is that clear?"

Nancy looked around the room. People were staring dumbly at their books, or at the backs of the people sitting in front of them. No one even glanced up.

"Good, well, let's move right along to participles."

How many years of this sort of thing had she sat through? She felt a twinge of anger as she thought of the hours she had spent simply turning off and retreating into a sort of mental paralysis. She looked around the room again. Were the others angry too? How did they cope? She noticed Roger Sam next to her. He was doodling on the lined paper in his notebook. Great spreading designs of vines that curled their way up the red margin filled the empty sheet with a profusion of leaves. He leaned forward, concentrating on the perfect tiny leaves that grew on the page. Elsie Jantzen kept capping and uncapping a chap stick. Jacob Worabey was playing with an eraser and some push pins. He had stuck four of them in the bottom and one as a head. An eraser pig! He had it prance around the top of his desk.

"And so," Donaldson was standing at the board pointing to some words written there, "you can see that 'thinking' and 'invented' are, no... Well, they modify nouns and so they're used as adjectives. Right? Notice carefully that they show action but do not serve as verbs in the sentences."

In front of her, Pauline McKay and Micky Joseph were giggling and kicking each other underneath their desks. Bob Sam and Lita Jack stared out the window. Nancy's mind drifted back up the river to her camp, and she heard the water chuckling through the rocks.

"So, what have we learned today?"

Nancy looked up at the clock. The period was almost over. What have we learned today? She thought. Well, that learning means sitting passively. That education means boredom. That English is irrelevant to our lives. That... The bell cut through her thoughts and she joined the rush for the door.

Her next class was chemistry and Charles Gordon, who always insisted on wearing a long white lab coat whether they were in the lab or not. He began lecturing as soon as the bell rang, and was so intent on the elaborate formulas on the board that he didn't even notice Nancy.

"Suppose we have here two products that decompose. Well, not decompose exactly. They have a forward reaction." He turned to the blackboard. "In this case we use $A + A$. Our back rate would be just as we've written before. So the equilibrium is reached where two substances have the same rate of reaction. So, K eg $= (x1)$ over $A2$. The rate is dependent on the number of collisions. The rate of collision increases as a square of the concentration. Now..." Suddenly he glowered over at Paul George who was whispering to Lita. He rapped on the board with his chalk. "I hope you realize this will be on your final exam, Mr. George." Caught, Paul sat upright and looked guiltily at the front of the room. "Now let's pay attention."

The tangled formulas stretched across the board, and Nancy thought about Mrs. Schmidt's nimble fingers weaving a basket, and she thought of racing the sun and growing strong.

By the time she got to algebra class, she had a sense of sitting in a very slow, very boring slide show. Each class was like a new slide, and each one gave the promise of being different, but only the background changed. There was the same voice in the front, the same straight rows of seats, the same listlessness among the students.

Lorraine Wells stood in front, pointing to equations on the board. "In these examples do you see that the greatest common factor of two or more polynomials is the common factor which in completely factored form has the greatest exponent and the greatest constant factor?" Mark Bateman nodded his head. "Good. So you can see that the least common multiple of the polynomials is the common multiple which in completely factored form has the least exponent and the least positive constant factor."

As the words droned on, Nancy felt the heat of the sweat, smelled the fir boughs, and heard the low voice of Mrs. Schmidt's chanting.

Nancy thought about leaving at lunch, but she was determined not to give up that easily. Besides, at least she could look forward to seeing Bernice last period. To get there she had to sit through social studies and a detailed lecture on the Powell-Sirois Commission that investigated provincial-federal relations in the late 1930s. Worst of all, she had to endure the baleful glares of Quigley in biology as he reviewed the structure of the cell. But she did endure it, though by the end she longed for the cool, quiet mornings and the sun-streaked evening sky.

Bernice looked up as Nancy walked through the home economics door, and the teacher's face lit up. She walked swiftly across the room and hugged Nancy. Then she stood back at arm's length and looked carefully at her.

"I heard you were back," she said. "You look great! It's so good to see you." She continued grinning. "Your eyes look so clear and bright. What have you been up to?"

"I've been studying with an elder."

"Yeah? That's great. Can you tell me about it later? Let me get the class going."

Bernice got the groups working on their projects by encouraging, not pushing, and soon the students were all engrossed. Bernice chatted with Nancy off and on, getting bits and pieces of the story between helping and listening to other students. She got more and more excited as the story unfolded. "Listen," she said finally, "let's get together so I can really concentrate. I've got a staff meeting this afternoon, so how about tomorrow after school? Our class is last period tomorrow again, isn't it?"

Nancy looked at the timetable taped to her notebook. "Yep. We have the same schedule tomorrow."

As class ended, Nancy began to think about George again. Her father said he had stopped over a couple of times while she'd been gone, but she hadn't seen him for a month and a half. When she'd come into town she'd tried to find him, but he wasn't at home. Friends said he hadn't been around much. He seemed to work then just disappear. She decided to walk to the mill and catch him there.

She climbed up to the highway and walked along the shoulder past the soccer field. On her right she could see the green field of the Ts'elht valley across the river. She traced the trail with her eyes and tried to imagine her sandy clearing hidden deep within the dense trees. Suddenly a huge truck blasted by, careening by her like a train on the bridge, blowing her hair in her eyes, and covering her in billowing dust and sand. Her heart pounded in her chest as she staggered to the side of the road and knelt on the sand.

Paying attention now to the highway, she completed the mile-long walk to the mill. "McDugan Forest Enterprises Ltd" read a big sign by the rutted road that dropped down to a long shed covered in corrugated steel. Stacks of lumber surrounded the long, low building, and a conveyor belt spit a steady stream of sawdust onto a pile that grew alongside. She could hear the low whine of the saws as she approached.

To her left, great fir logs were stacked like the bones of huge animals. A lift was prying them out and bringing them to a log deck where they were kicked onto a carriage. As she watched they went through a series of saws and chains and rollers until they were spewed out at the end as long white boards, still sticky with sap and smelling of life.

She spotted George at the far end of the shed, with three other guys, all wearing hard hats and ear guards. They were pulling the sawed boards off the green chain and stacking them on blocks. Around them piles of brown slabs were accumulating to be hauled away and burned. She glanced around as she approached. The ground was still muddy in places, and the loaders had chewed the dirt up into a swamp. Old pieces of machinery and coils of cable sat rusting around the mill. The scream of the saws became more deafening as she got closer.

As Nancy reached the bottom of the road and began crossing toward the mill George looked around and saw her. He threw the board he was lifting on a pile, yelled something to someone beside him, and walked toward Nancy.

He wasn't more than twenty feet from the green chain when Bud McDugan lunged out of the office, a tiny plywood building beside the mill. He leaped over logs, strips of bark, and mud puddles till he got behind George. George still had on his ear guards and didn't hear a thing until McDugan grabbed him by the shoulder and spun him around.

She saw George knock McDugan's hand away, then turn around full to face him. His legs were spread as if to brace himself. Nancy couldn't hear the whole conversation, but bits and pieces floated over the screeching of the saws. "I don't care... You're working for me... If you don't like... There are plenty of other guys who... better watch your step, mister... not running a dating service here and..."

Finally George turned away angrily, leaving McDugan still muttering behind him.

"Geez, George, I didn't mean to cause any trouble for you."

George's face was flushed, but he dismissed it with a shrug. "Forget it. That guy's such a dork he thinks we should get permission from him when we go to the can. This place is worse than school."

"Could you lose your job?" Nancy asked anxiously.

George shrugged again. "I've given this guy four years of my labour. I wonder how much he's made off me? Maybe it's time to move on anyway. Hey, how are you?"

George reached out his long arms and hugged her. She tilted her face up to his and they kissed.

"Geez, I've missed you," George whispered. "When can we talk?"

"I'll meet you at the Corral after work. When do you get done?"

George glanced at his watch. "In about an hour." He kissed her again and smiled. "I'll see you then."

It took her a half hour to make her way back to the school, then down the hill into Creighton. Sitting in a corner as far away from the babble and chatter of the video games and students as she could, she stared out the window at Grebs' store and thought about her father and about the cold surging stream that wore the rocks smooth in her pool.

George's truck pulled up in front of the cafe and he walked slowly inside. He saw her, smiled, and walked over.

"So how you doing?" He seemed almost shy. "Your father told me about Mrs. Schmidt and your quest. How was it?"

Nancy began relating her experiences, and slowly George began to relax. She talked about Mrs. Schmidt's teaching and what she had learned. She told him about the sweats and the chanting, the bathing, the running, and through it all George listened intently. At the end there was a long silence. Finally he reached out his hand and covered hers.

"I'm really happy for you. You're a different person from when

113

you left. Even I can see that." He paused. "I think I have a lot of catching up to do."

"How have you been doing?" she asked gently.

"Me, oh, you know. I'm doing OK. Did you hear about the old Indian guy whose youngest son manages to get through high school and goes to college? Well, he comes home after the first semester and the father says, 'Tell me one thing you've learned so I can tell everyone about how smart you're getting.' Well the kid thinks for a while and says, 'πr^2'. The old man holds his head in his hands and moans, 'My God, this is what we send you to college for? Pie aren't squared, cakes are squared. Pies are round'."

Nancy smiled, and George smiled back, but it was thin and didn't last long. There was no sparkle in his eyes.

"You haven't been at home or around town much. Where have you been?"

George looked down at the napkin he was twisting in his lap. "Oh, I don't know. Down by the graveyard I guess. I sit a lot by Barry's grave trying to figure things out." His voice cracked, and he squeezed his eyes with his fingers. "Things just haven't been the same since he died."

Nancy reached over and held his other hand. "You know, one thing I learned is that it's OK to cry, and I did a lot of it."

George looked up and managed a slow smile. "So have I. Maybe I'm learning in my own way. But what are you doing?" He nodded at her books. "Are you back at school?"

"Yeah," Nancy said. "For a while. You know I never realized how stifling things were up there. When I was learning from Mrs. Schmidt and on my quest, it was all so different. It was real, and it was mine directly. It made me feel stronger, more powerful. It seemed natural and part of the surroundings. But at the school it all comes through the teachers. You leave feeling weaker, not stronger. And so little of it has anything to do with me. Most of the teachers seem distant, more interested in their subjects than us."

"I know," George agreed. "Why do you think I left?"

"And today, watching everyone, it was almost frightening. We were all just sitting there acting the way we've been told to. There's no real discussion, no thinking about our situations and problems. No action. There's no risk. No decisions. Nobody has to think about even the smallest things. We just do what we're told, think what we're told. It's no wonder people are all gimped up when they leave.

Maybe the ones who get out early are the smart ones."

George shook his head. "Leaving's not much of a solution either. First of all when you leave you feel bad about yourself—you're a failure. Somehow you never shake that. It lives inside you. And then, what can you do? That diploma does open doors."

"Somehow the school has to change, that's all there is to it. There are more ways and more things to learn than what's up there now."

"But what can you do?" George asked.

Now Nancy shook her head. "I don't know, but I guess tomorrow I'll find out."

XIV.

The next morning Doughnut was waiting for her. She stood outside the glass cage of the office, her arms folded over her chest, scrutinizing the students as they came through the door. When she spotted Nancy, she raised her hand and pointed at her, palm down, over the heads of the other students. Nancy walked through the crowd.

"Did you want to see me?"

"I certainly did," Doughnut snapped. "Step into the office."

Nancy followed Doughnut through the open door, noticing the sweet smell of powder and perfume that drifted behind her. Doughnut quickly walked behind the counter and faced Nancy.

"Miss Antoine, you really do have a lot of gall. You have been out of school for nearly two months, and then you just waltz back in here like you own the place. No excuse. No explanation. Nothing. You didn't even check in yesterday." She paused, her lips pressed into a thin, severe line. "Well, what do you have to say?"

"Six weeks," Nancy said.

"What?"

"Six weeks. I was gone for six weeks."

"Six weeks, eight weeks," Doughnut said waving her hand, "that's not the point. I think, Miss Antoine, you should have a little chat with Mr. Patterson. 3:30 this afternoon," she finished curtly.

"A chat with Mr. Patterson," Nancy mused. "Yes, that sounds like a good idea. There really are some things I'd like to talk with him about. That should be fine, 3:30." She turned and went to the door, noticing a look of puzzlement cross Doughnut's face as if things hadn't gone exactly as intended.

English class began just as hundreds had before. The students sat quietly while Mr. Donaldson carefully ticked their names off in his blue attendance book. Then he closed it, carefully set it aside, and opened the grammar book.

"Would you turn to page 390 in your book today." The class obediently took out their books and opened them. A few people groaned, but Mr. Donaldson didn't seem to hear them.

"Today we're continuing with our discussion on verbals, but now we're going to focus on gerunds, or verbal nouns. It seems strange to think of a verb as a noun, doesn't it?"

Roger Sam was already working on his doodles. Today they looked like mice mounting an attack on a castle.

"Now a gerund is an 'ing' form of the verb that is used as a noun. It can be the object of a preposition, a subject, a direct object, a predicate nominative, or an appositive."

"Mr. Donaldson," Nancy said. "Is this necessary?"

Mr. Donaldson looked like someone had kicked him in the stomach. There was a silence as every doodling pencil stopped and every drooping eye snapped open. There was a long silence, and everyone stared at Nancy wide-eyed as though she'd sprouted antennae and green scales.

"I mean, isn't English a way of communicating?"

An indecipherable gurgle came from Mr. Donaldson as he nervously tugged at the cuffs of his green jacket.

"Then why don't we communicate? Why don't we write and talk about things that are important to us? Wouldn't that be a better way to learn English?"

Mr. Donaldson seemed to be recovering from his paralysis. "Nancy," he said patiently, "English is like a puzzle. You have to know the pieces before you can put the puzzle together."

Nancy shook her head. "I'm not so sure about that. You seem to think we learn all the bits and then somehow we can figure out how to put them together. But when an Indian woman teaches you to tan a hide, you watch the whole thing. Then the smaller jobs make sense because you see how they fit into the whole task."

"English is not hide tanning, Nancy," Mr. Donaldson said.

"Anyway, we need to learn some grammar," said Betsy Vanklassen.

"Maybe some." Jacob Worabey had turned in his seat near the front to speak to the others. "But do you remember all this stuff?" There was emphatic head shaking and someone muttered "Hardly."

"So maybe we'd be better off writing more and seeing what sort of grammar we need."

Mr. Donaldson looked paler than usual. His eyes seemed big and round. "Do you know how long it takes to mark a set of essays?" he asked. "There are 30 of you in here. That means hours and hours of marking."

"Well then," offered Jacob, "maybe we should have smaller classes."

"Yeah," said Pauline McKay, "or maybe there are ways we can write for each other."

Donaldson thumped his book. "Class," he squeaked, "this is getting entirely out of hand."

"Out of hand?" Jacob asked. "This is the first real discussion we've had in this class since September."

As the debate went on, Nancy watched the students carefully. Though a few were opening up and saying what they thought, most still sat back silent, a look of fear or confusion on their faces. Some seemed angry.

"I think Mr. Donaldson is our teacher," declared Jane McDugan, "and he knows what's best for us."

"Thank you, Jane," Donaldson said, trying to get his class back. "I'd like you to turn to the exercises on page 391."

The students, seeing the issue closed, turned reluctantly back to their books. But there was a stirring of defiance in the air.

Nancy wondered if it was really there or if she only imagined it. In chemistry Mr. Gordon was standing up front in his lab coat. "So if you increase the molarity you increase the total number of molecules in that solution, and there are, of course, a greater number of collisions."

He pointed to an equation on the board. "In this one I've only put one substance here. This will be raised to the second power. And this one will be raised to the second power. So this will be the equilibrium quotient."

"Mr. Gordon, why are we doing this?"

Gordon stopped and looked at her. He had always seemed like a reasonable guy, so she was interested in his answer.

"For the test, of course. All this material will be on the final test. And it's all covered on the provincial exams as well."

"Geez, Mr. Gordon," Paul George said, "you know, this stuff drives me crazy. I learn enough to pass the tests..."

"Sometimes," someone said, and the class chuckled.

"...but then I just forget it. It all seems so meaningless."

"Yeah," agreed Jacob, "I don't remember half the stuff we learned at the beginning of the year."

"Well you better," Gordon shot back. "'Cause it's going to be on the exam."

"You know, Mr. Gordon," Jacob said angrily, "I don't think that's a good enough answer. I mean, how is this going to affect us, our lives?"

"I'll tell you how," Mr. Gordon said loudly. "If you don't pass the test then you flunk the course and you don't graduate. Now that's enough of this."

Jacob slammed his book shut. Several others muttered, and there was a sulleness in the room as the instructor glared at them. "And if there's any more of this some of you are going to find yourselves right out of here."

By the third period there was a new sense of expectancy in the air, an edge, a growing anger.

"OK, let's look at a few problems now." Lorraine Wells was standing at her desk. "Let's say a private art collector buys a painting but has to sell it to a museum because of a depression or something at a ten percent loss. Some years later he buys it back at an auction and resells it to another museum for $42,000 more than the auction price. If the gallery made a 25 percent profit and the collector made a 39.5 percent net profit on his original investment, for what price did he originally buy the picture? Now, how do we put that into an equation? Let's say the original price is X, then..."

"Miss Wells," Nancy began quietly. "I've always had a hard time relating to algebra. Does anyone ever use it?"

The teacher looked uncertainly around the room. "Well, sure. Engineers and scientists use it all the time. Why, I use it every day." She gave a small smile.

"But I'm not going to be an engineer," Lita blurted out. "How come I've got to take this?"

Mark Bateman turned around and glared at her. "Well, I am, and I think it's important."

"Great," said Lorraine Adams, "you take it then. But what about us?"

"You know, it's not just for practical reasons that you take algebra," Wells said. "It's excellent mental discipline. It makes you think more clearly and precisely."

"Well maybe that's what we should be emphasizing then," said Nancy.

The clamor and debate continued until the bell for lunch. Immediately Nancy noticed Miss Wells hurry down to the staff room, a look of determination on her face that implied more than mid-day hunger.

At lunch there was a buzz of excitement. Students sat in clusters and eagerly talked about what had happened in the morning. Soon Jacob Worabey came up to Nancy, smiling.

"You know, I think you've really started something. It's spreading all over the school." He paused. "Where do you think it'll end?"

In social studies, Nancy didn't even start off. In the middle of Zachary Taylor's lecture Cyril Narcisse broke in.

"Couldn't we do something else rather than all these lectures?"

"Yeah" Pauline agreed. "How about group projects? I'll remember how to find out information longer than I'll recall all these facts."

"And how about studying our own community for a change?" Nancy looked in astonishment at the speaker. It was Big John Joseph. In all the years she had been in school Nancy never remembered him saying more than a few words. She nodded encouragement as he looked at her shyly. "I mean, that seems more important to me. What about that idea of doing something on the bridge?"

"I think history is important," Jerry Weiss said. "How can we know where we're going if we don't know where we've been?"

"OK, but when do we get to study our lives, our problems, and do something about them?" asked John in his deep, hushed voice. Nancy could hardly believe it. John had actually argued for his point of view.

"How about land claims," somebody shouted. "Why don't we study that?"

"Yeah," said someone else, "or how to stop lumber companies from logging the Ts'elht."

"Or better yet, have different groups working on different projects," someone else called out.

Suddenly the class grew quiet. Nancy glanced over at the door to see Doughnut standing there, stern and impatient. She was looking directly at Nancy.

"Miss Antoine, Mr. Patterson would like to see you in his office."

"But my appointment isn't until 3:30."

"Now, Miss Antoine," Doughnut replied crisply.

Nancy got out of her seat and walked down the hall. She could hear students chattering and calling out questions as she passed open doors. She followed Doughnut into the office and behind the counter to the principal's office. The secretary knocked on the door.

"Yes?"

"Mr. Patterson," Doughnut said, opening the door a crack. "Miss Antoine is here."

"Yes. Send her in."

Doughnut stood aside, holding the door open by the knob. She looked down her nose as Nancy walked into the inner office. Inside, Mr. Patterson, a small, chubby man with thinning brown hair, sat in a swivel chair behind a big steel desk. A small sign on the desk read "Mr. N. Patterson, Principal." He was reading papers in an open folder as she entered and didn't look up.

Nancy sat down in an orange upholstered chair slightly to one side of the desk and heard the door click shut behind her. Staring out the window behind the principal, she could see the two rivers swirling around Tschweh mountain, colliding as they reached the point.

Finally Mr. Patterson put down his papers and pushed his heavy black glasses up his long nose. She felt his stare as he studied her with his pale blue eyes and turned to face him. Meeting his gaze she was surprised to find that there was no fear in her, no need to avert her eyes or to cower away from his stare as she had the last time she had been here. That time she'd been one of four Indian students who had come to ask about forming an Indian student club. She remembered how he had sat eyeing them coldly while they stood fidgeting in front of his desk. Nancy had trembled with fear and had been unable to speak. She remembered, too, his response after they had haltingly explained their request.

"Now, we don't want to call attention to any one group, do we?" he had said, peering through those thick glasses. "We don't want to single one group out as being different, do we? We all want to treat everyone the same here. We want to be one big happy family." His smile was as cold as his eyes.

"Sure, we're all the same in lots of ways," Nancy had managed to stammer, "but we're different too."

Mr. Patterson had frowned. "The matter's closed. No Native club. No Ukrainian club. No Chinese club. We're trying to promote integration and uniformity here, not separation and differences. Those things are divisive. There's no place for them in this school."

"But three quarters of the school is Indian," another student had pleaded, "and there's nothing here that's Indian. Not the courses, the teachers, the way the school is run..."

Patterson had stood up, glaring. "The matter is closed. You may go now."

Today, it was different. He seemed to watch her warily, and Nancy felt calm and at ease.

"Nancy, I've called you in here because I'm getting some disturbing reports from the teachers. Now, listen Nancy, I want you to stop all these disruptions."

"Disruptions? What disruptions? All I'm doing is asking some questions."

Mr. Patterson slammed his hand down on the desk. "You know what I mean," he said. He sat back in his chair and seemed to consciously restrain himself. He smiled ingratiatingly and leaned forward. Nancy noticed that her name was on the folder open on the desk.

"Now Nancy, let's be reasonable. You've spent a lot of time in this school. It would be a real shame to throw all that away." He pushed his glasses up his nose again and pointed to her file. "Among other things, it appears that you've been gone nearly two months."

"Six weeks," said Nancy.

"Yes, ah, six weeks. That's really a very long time. Normally that would jeopardize a student's school year." He sat back again, his eyes narrowed shrewdly. "However, I think I can say with confidence, in fact I can guarantee it, that we can overlook this little attendance problem and give you your diploma."

Nancy watched him carefully.

"Now that's very reasonable of us, don't you think?"

"What are you suggesting, Mr. Patterson?"

Patterson pushed his face closer toward her. "I'm suggesting that if you quit this troublemaking and go back to being a quiet, reasonable student again, you'll graduate. And if you don't, well, you have missed an awful lot of school."

"Yes, Mr. Patterson, I have missed a lot of school. But during that time I've done more learning than I have here in the last twelve years." She paused. "That diploma used to mean more to me than anything else in the world. It was my way out of this town, this nightmare."

"But Nancy," Mr. Patterson said soothingly, "it still can be."

"No. It just isn't that important anymore. I'll get my grade twelve if I need it — there are other routes than this one. But there's too much at stake here to sell it out for a slip of paper."

Patterson planted his hands on the desk and stood up. "This is my school," he growled, "and I'm not going to let you or anyone else sabotage it."

"How much did the Department of Indian Affairs put into this building?" Nancy asked. "And what percent of the operating budget is federal money paid as tuition for native students? This isn't your school. It's ours. But somehow, like a lot of other things, you ended up with it."

"Those matters are none of your concern," snarled the principal. "I'll put it to you straight. Either you conform to the rules and regulations of this school or you get out. Do I make myself clear? And if you don't get out on your own, I'll have you thrown out!"

Now Nancy stood up. She looked at the red-faced man shaking with rage and, just maybe, a faint sense of helplessness. She almost felt sorry for his desperate need for control. The whole thing, she thought, is a house of cards. It only stands up as long as nobody asks questions. As soon as someone does, it begins to shake and tremble.

"You know," Nancy said, "we flunk out or are forced out of this school four times as often as white students. Did you ever wonder why? Why we have flunked twice on average by the time we get to grade ten, if we're lucky to get that far? Why we're stuck in those technical training programs and are ten times less likely to win academic awards? Did you *ever* wonder about those things when you were holed up here behind your desk? And when you do force us out, we leave feeling that we are the failures. That way you get rid of the problems and no one ever points the finger at you, right? Well, this is one Indian you're not forcing out. If you want me out, you'll have to drag me out."

Nancy's voice never rose. There was no anger, no fear. She stated it all calmly, with clear, strong emphasis. As she stood there, she felt her heart pulsing softly, slowly.

There was a silence. Then the principal pointed to the door. "Get out," he hissed. "Get out of my office and out of my school. And if you want me to throw you out, I can arrange that too. Believe me, Miss Antoine, you can't win this one. I'm stronger and more powerful than you'll ever be."

Nancy smiled slightly and looked at him almost gently. "The sad thing, Mr. Patterson, is that you don't even know what strength and power really are. You've been dealing in fear and control for so long that you've gotten them all confused. It's too bad."

Nancy turned and walked to the door. Just as she was leaving she turned back to the principal. "You know, Mr. Patterson, I know some people who could teach you a good deal, I think."

"Get out!" he screamed. "Now!"

Nancy slipped through the door and out through the office. Doughnut was sitting at her typewriter. As Nancy passed, she gave Doughnut a smile and a little wave.

Classes had changed since she had gone to see the principal. She headed for her next class—biology and Quigley. As she passed through the halls she felt a tension spilling from the classrooms. She sensed the eyes of students on her as she walked toward the biology room.

As she entered, Quigley glared at her from underneath his thick eyebrows, but he said nothing. She made her way to her seat behind Big John Joseph. A diagram of a cell was drawn on the board.

"As I was saying," rumbled Quigley, "inside the cell is the cytoplasm. Now, what's inside this cytoplasm?" There was an expectant silence in the room. The students stole glances at Nancy, but she sat still, looking at the board. "Well?" Quigley asked sharply. "You should all remember this from the fall when we studied it. Tom Charlie, name some of the parts of a cell." His voice rose in exasperation, but Tom sat staring at his desk.

"Come on, come on," Quigley continued. "There's the nucleus, of course. What about the Golgi apparatus? The mitochondria? The vacuoles?" His voice rose as the silence deepened.

Nobody stirred. Quigley continued to glare around the class.

"Mr. Quigley," Nancy's low voice cut through the room like a knife. There was a sharp intake of breath as the students watched. "We seem to spend all our time trying to break the world into tinier and tinier pieces."

"Of course," snapped Quigley, "that's the basis of the reductionist approach."

"Well, I don't know about that, but wouldn't it make more sense if we also studied the unity of things? How they're all part of a single, you know, system? How we are part of the whole?"

"Don't try any of your impertinence with me, young lady. I've taken five years of university science. I think I am in a position to determine the correct approach."

"That's another thing," Nancy began. Some of the students had begun to smile, but they still eyed Quigley with fear. "How about some field trips? Biology is the study of life. Why don't we get out into it and experience it directly?"

Quigley stepped from around the desk and stalked toward Nancy. His face seemed to get redder and redder as he got closer. "How dare you tell me how to teach? I've taught for twenty-two years and I'm not going to let some, some Indian tell me what to do with my classroom!" His rage seemed to mount as he advanced down the aisle. He had his hand out as if to grab her. Nancy sat calmly as Quigley approached. Another few feet and he'd have her.

Suddenly Big John Joseph stood up and took one step sideways. He stood a head taller than Quigley, and his body filled the space between the rows. "Don't touch her." His voice was low and soft, but there was a menace there, too, that wasn't lost even on Quigley.

He staggered back one step, staring wildly at John, the class, then Nancy. Speechless, he whirled around and rushed past the front of the class to the door. "You haven't seen the end of this," he spit, as he raked them all with his blazing little eyes. Then he was gone.

There was a long silence in the room. Then Jacob Worabey muttered, "Hooray for Dorothy. The wicked witch is dead."

Everybody laughed, but there was nervousness too. People looked apprehensively at the door as the bell rang.

"What do we do now?" someone asked.

Nancy stood up. "I don't know about you, but I'm going to my next class."

The students filed out into the hall. Nancy could see them whispering about what had happened, their heads together in little knots of excitement. As she walked by one group, she saw Mary George hold up her fingers in a "V".

"I heard you and Patterson had it out," Mary said.

"How did you hear that?" Nancy asked.

Mary shrugged. "What are they going to do next?"

Nancy smiled wryly. "You got me. But I don't expect to be here long."

"If you go, we all go," promised Mary. "And we won't come back."

When Nancy walked into the home economics class, Bernice was waiting, concern written across her face.

"My God, Nancy," she said, "what have you been up to? They're really after you. I thought Quigley was going to have a heart attack."

"Yeah, I know. Mrs. Schmidt was right. There are times to be quiet and times to ask questions. This seemed like a time to ask some questions."

"I'm not so sure," Bernice said worriedly. "I think this may have been one of those other times."

Bernice began the class and people started working at the counters, but there was a low hum of excited conversation around the cutting boards. Jacob and Rose Jack worked on moose ragout, a recipe they'd adapted from one they'd found in an international cookbook.

Jacob chopped onions and wiped his eyes. "Well, this has certainly been an interesting day."

"It's not over yet." Rose said. "Look." She pointed her knife at the door. Constable Thiessen, flanked by two other RCMPs, stood in the hall outside the room. He was conferring quietly with Mr. Patterson. Thiessen stepped forward, his bulk blocking the doorway. Mr. Patterson's plump hand reached over the constable's shoulder and pointed a pudgy finger at Nancy. Thiessen put his hands on his belt, adjusted his holster, and swaggered toward her.

Before he could take two steps, a small figure stepped in his way.

"May I help you?" Bernice asked, holding her ground despite Thiessen's size. He continued walking until he was only inches from her. He hitched his thumbs in his belt and stared down at the slight woman in front of him.

"You the teacher?" Thiessen grunted.

"That's right."

"I've been asked to remove one of your students."

"By what authority?" Bernice asked angrily. She actually managed to lean forward until her nose was almost touching his chin. Thiessen, obviously unaccustomed to being confronted, looked around uneasily.

"Section IV, paragraph 13 of the School Act authorizes a principal to designate any person on school premises as a trespasser and have that person removed. That's what I'm doing. I'm just enforcing the law."

"Nancy's no trespasser," Bernice protested. "She's a student here."

"Not according to Mr. Patterson. I'm acting at his request."

"Well, you'll have to come through me to get her." Bernice put her hands on her hips and glared at Thiessen. It was like a picture Nancy had once seen of a tiny kitten arching its back and spitting at a Great Dane.

Thiessen pushed his stomach out and stood up even straighter. "Listen lady, if you want to get charged with obstruction, keep this up. You're mighty close now."

Nancy put down her knife and slipped off her apron. "It's OK, Bernice. I'll go. I don't want to make any trouble for you."

She walked toward Thiessen and looked up at his closed face, his eyes still glaring at Bernice. "Come on. Let's go."

Behind her she heard a knife slam down. "Not alone, you're not." Rose walked up behind her.

"Right," said Jacob, and then she heard others putting down their utensils and taking off aprons. She moved out into the hall. Thiessen started to lead her toward the back door. Nancy pulled down the hall the other way.

"I have to go upstairs to get my things out of my locker," she explained.

Thiessen looked uncertainly at the students crowding around. "OK, but make it snappy."

As Nancy walked down the hall, she glanced over her shoulder. Almost the entire home economics class was behind her, and other students, who had probably seen the police when they'd entered, were streaming out of other classrooms. As she climbed the stairs she heard the chant rising behind her: "Out! Out! Out!"

When she reached the first floor, students were already standing in the doorways. They fell in behind as she walked. Big John Joseph strode up beside her without saying a word and stationed himself to her right. Jacob Worabey moved to her left. As she passed her locker, she decided its contents were unimportant now.

"Out! Out! Out!" People were hammering the lockers in unison and the chant crashed through the halls. More and more students, some looking grim, some scared, some triumphant, walked out of classrooms and joined the crowd behind her.

They passed by the last classroom and then by the office. Doughnut was standing behind the glass, her fist pressed to her mouth and her eyes round with horror. Nancy walked through the double doors and into the sunlight. She continued on until she had reached the road. Then she stopped and turned around. A hundred students were crowding around her, and still more were straggling out the door. Most were Indian, but there were white faces, too.

Jacob leaned over. "What now?" he whispered.

Nancy shook her head. "I don't know. I didn't really plan on all this, you know."

Jacob looked at the people still chanting "Out! Out! Out!" He rolled his eyes. "Well, we'd better get a plan together," he said. The students behind them seemed stunned, with a look of astonishment on their faces as though they had completed some impossible task. Then, slowly, they quieted and looked toward him and Nancy. "And we'd better hurry," he added.

XV.

The Corral became strike headquarters. The next day the students circulated in and out, filling up the tables with coke cans and discussing their plans. After the initial rush of the walkout, the cold reality of what they had done began to sink in. About a third of the students had not walked out. They told the strikers that Patterson had called them together in the gym and told them that unless the others returned by the end of the week, the strikers would all lose credit for the year and those in grade twelve wouldn't graduate.

"Can he do that?" asked Roger Charlie, who was hoping to go on into a fisheries program in the fall.

"Naw, I don't think so," assured Jacob. "He's just trying to bluff us." But there was a note of uncertainty in his voice, and Nancy could see the worry growing in Roger's eyes.

"What exactly are we striking for?" asked Charlotte Adams. "I mean, don't people always have definite demands when they strike?"

"We should demand that they start an Indian studies program," someone called out.

"What does that mean?" Bobby McKay demanded. "Traditional stuff like hide tanning and basket making? Spirituality? Or things about what it's like to be an Indian now and what skills we need today?"

"I don't know, maybe some of both."

"Why bother? They'll just teach it like all the other courses."

"I think we need a Shuswap language program."

"Well listen, we've gotta learn the stuff we need so we can make it outside, too."

"Like what?"

"Math, English, that kinda thing."

"But it's more important that we learn what we need here in this community. This is where we live."

"All I know," Lita Adams said quietly, "is that if you come out feeling crumby about yourself at the end then it doesn't matter what they've taught."

"Yeah, and you gotta learn how to think, not just copy notes off the board."

"But look," broke in Roger, "we need programs that are going to

131

get us ready to take vocational courses so we can get jobs."

"What about stuff you need for university? I want to be a teacher."

"The most important thing to me," Big John Joseph said slowly, "is to learn what it means to be Indian. I want to feel good about me and being Indian."

There was a long pause. "Geez, this isn't going to be easy," muttered Lita, who had taken out a piece of paper to jot down their demands.

Nancy looked around the circle of discouraged faces. "Why should it be easy? We're all different and have different ideas about what schools should be and what we need. Why should we agree any more than anyone else? We can't hassle all this out now, but one thing is clear. We need to get to the people who can make changes. We need to have a showdown with the school board and the superintendent. We've got to get them here and listen to us. Patterson will never change. We've got to go over his head."

"So how do we do that?"

"Somebody's got to call and ask the superintendent, I guess."

"Well, who's going to call?"

Everyone looked at Nancy. "Why me?" she asked. "I'm not any leader."

"Maybe not, but since you've come back you're different," said Cyril Narcisse. "You can say things we think but are afraid to say. You do it."

So Nancy walked to the pay phone in the corner and dialed the school board office. She asked for Harry Dworkin, the superintendent, and after several minutes, he finally came on the other end.

"Mr. Dworkin," Nancy began, "I am one of the students here in Creighton who walked out. I guess you heard about that?"

"You must be Nancy Antoine," Dworkin replied. "Yes, Mr. Patterson informed me that there was some problem."

"Well, it's more than some problem. It's a lot of problems. And we would like to talk to you about our complaints and see if we can make things better here."

The phone seemed to go dead for a moment as if the superintendent had put his hand over the receiver. She could hear muffled voices but couldn't make out what was being said.

Finally Dworkin came back on the line. "Yes. Well, Miss Antoine, I'm not in the habit of negotiating with students. I'm afraid that you are dealing with the wrong person. My advice is to go back to classes and then take up your complaints with the administration of your school. Mr. Patterson is a reasonable man."

"But Mr. Dworkin, we..."

"I'm sorry, Nancy; that's my final word. I think it is only fair of me to remind you that all of you who continue to stay away from classes are jeopardizing your year. I might also mention that disciplinary action, including dismissal, may be considered for those who do not attend classes," he paused for effect, "and especially those who seem to be encouraging this behavior. You think about it Miss Antoine."

The phone went dead in her hand. She slowly put it back on the hook and returned to the students who were looking expectantly at her.

"Well?" Cyril asked.

Nancy looked around. Time was obviously against them; the school could simply sit back and wait. One by one the students would drift back and the strike would collapse with nothing gained and people feeling even more powerless than before.

"Well what?" Nancy asked, her eyes flashing. "We didn't expect them to give in with the first shove, did we? Now it's time to organize. We've got to pressure those guys to meet with us."

"How?"

How? thought Nancy. "First of all we've got to get the press here. T.V. and radio and newspapers. Then we have to get the parents, the community on our side. We have to explain why we've walked out. We'll make so much noise they can't ignore us."

People smiled and cheered with relief. Finally there was a focus. There was something to do.

Then Nancy noticed Lonnie Thomas walk in through the cafe door. He wore shiny new cowboy boots, a satiny western shirt with pearl buttons, and a beige sport coat. His jeans were pressed in a sharp crease down the front of each leg. Lonnie was from the reserve and worked as the home-school coordinator. He was supposed to help students who had problems with the school but usually he drank coffee in the staff room and only talked with students to warn them about attendance or behavior. What does he want? Nancy wondered.

He walked up to the circle of students and smiled broadly. His wispy mustache hung down over his gleaming teeth.

"Hey guys, what's happening?" he asked brightly. There was a long silence as people eyed him suspiciously.

He cleared his throat nervously. "Hey, I heard there was a little trouble, so I hurried right down here to see if I could, you know, help work things out."

"Whose side are you on?" Cyril asked, punching a straw through a styrofoam cup. "Did Patterson send you?"

"Hey, we're all on the same side here, right? We all want you guys to get a good education. I'm just here to help patch up the misunderstandings and get you guys back in school where you belong. Listen, I've been working on this and I think I've got Mr. Patterson ready to meet with you guys if you'll come back. Hey, I can't guarantee anything, but maybe we can even get him to agree to a native studies program. What do you think of that?"

There was no response. Cyril kept poking holes in the cup.

"So what'ya say? Let's forget all this and, ha ha, bury the tomahawk."

Cyril stopped poking the cup. "Hey Lonnie, I got one question for you. Are you an Indian?"

Lonnie laughed a high nervous laugh. His curly black hair glistened. "Hey, what kinda question is that?" His laughter trailed away until he stood silent, awkwardly shifting his weight from foot to foot.

"Go on, Lonnie," Cyril continued. "We've got work to do. And tell Patterson that we'll talk about coming back after we meet with the school board and superintendent. Not before."

Lonnie's smile faded away and his face became sullen and hard. "Who do you guys think you are? Who are you to demand anything? I'm gonna give you a piece of advice and you better listen good. If I were you I'd get back in that school fast. Right now they're still not too mad. They may let you back in. But if you continue this stupid little protest much longer you're in big trouble."

Big John Joseph stood up and began walking toward Lonnie, his thumbs hooked in his belt. "You better go now," he said, moving forward threateningly.

Lonnie took a step back. "OK, OK, have it your own way. Throw away your education. But you haven't seen anything yet. This is gonna get nasty." He gave a dark sneer. "You guys are pathetic. You actually think you can bring the school down?" He stalked away, giving the door a vicious shove on the way out.

There was an uncomfortable silence after he left. "Maybe he's right," someone muttered. "Maybe we're just kidding ourselves."

"Maybe he *is* right," Nancy said quietly. "I don't know what we can do either. But we haven't even tried yet. Do you want to give up now and slink back to school?"

Big John, always so soft-spoken before, stopped walking back to his chair and turned to stare at the group. "Not me," he said. "If I go down this time, I do it fighting. I'm tired of being stepped on and feeling weak. I've got nothing to lose."

"Right," someone called. "Let's get to work." There were shouts of agreement, and Nancy felt the tension break. The excitement and momentum was there again. But for how long? They had to force a showdown quickly.

They broke the community up into sections and teams of students formed to go to each house on the reserve. The few white students agreed to try to explain the situation to the white community.

"Good luck," someone muttered.

Jacob smiled. "Look, we can go back to that school tomorrow and there will be no problem. Or we can go to another school that looks just like this one. You're the guys fighting for your lives. It doesn't really matter if we succeed or not. What's critical is that you get the Indian community behind you. Without that you're done for."

Nancy agreed to contact the media. She called the local television station and asked for the news director.

"A hundred Indian students walked out of Creighton High?" the woman gasped. "Are you sure?"

Nancy laughed. "I'm sitting with about a quarter of them now."

"We'll have a camera crew out there in an hour."

That night Nancy watched herself on television for the first time, explaining the situation to the newswoman. The interview had been conducted in front of the Corral, and behind them the cafe's logo — the bronc rider bouncing above his horse — was painted on the glass. On television it looked like the cowboy was putting his hat on Nancy's head. Next time, she thought, we'll do our interviews somewhere else.

She was sitting at George's with a group of other strikers. "How do you think I did?" Nancy asked anxiously.

"Great," George said, "except your zipper was down on your jeans."

Nancy's eyes grew wide. "It was not! Was it?"

Everybody laughed, and Nancy batted George playfully on the shoulder. "Geez George, that's nasty."

"Is that all the coverage we get?" someone asked. "What's going to happen now?"

The next morning the town was crawling with newspeople who sensed a larger issue. Four newspapers, two radio stations, and three television stations, including the CBC, had reporters combing Creighton for anyone involved in the walkout.

"What should we say?" Mary McKay asked.

"Say anything you want," Nancy answered. "But remember what we want: a meeting with the school board and superintendent. Make it clear we're willing to talk; they're the ones who're refusing to negotiate."

Nancy talked until she was hoarse, and that night the news reports were full of the strike. Even Big John Joseph got on television. He watched himself on George's set and a big grin spread across his face.

"Are you one of the strikers," a young interviewer was asking John while pushing a microphone in his face.

"Yep," said John.

"And do you want a meeting with the school board?"

"Uh huh."

"And what do you want to say to them?"

"Things need to change," John answered.

"This must be pretty exciting, eh?" asked the woman, a note of exasperation creeping into her voice.

"Yep," said Big John.

"Geez," John said, "I've never seen myself on T.V. before."

"You look great," George said, "but next time you gotta remember to talk."

The next morning, Nancy was at the Corral with a group of students working on plans to picket the school. Shortly after the telephone rang, Leo Gamboni, the Corral's owner, called from behind the counter. "Nancy, it's for you."

Nancy walked over to the counter and Leo handed her the phone. "Listen," he said, "I don't mind you turning my restaurant into an office, but if you're going to start taking calls here, how about having a business line put in over there in the corner?"

Nancy put the phone to her ear. "Hello."

"Miss Antoine, this is Mrs. Loretta Lewis. I am Mr. Dworkin's secretary." She had the same cold, efficient voice Doughnut had.

Nancy wondered if they learned that in secretarial school.

"Yes."

"I'm calling to arrange a meeting. Mr. Dworkin will meet with you and a small group of students, no more than five, in the principal's office at Creighton High at 8:30 tonight."

Nancy thought quickly. "Tell Mr. Dworkin that we're pleased he's agreed to meet with us," Nancy paused, "and the time's fine. But we'll only meet if whoever is interested can come." There was a sharp intake of breath on the other end. "And we'll meet at the pow wow grounds next to the band hall."

There was a long silence, then a hand was placed over the receiver. Nancy thought she could hear Dworkin's voice in the background, but she couldn't be sure.

After what seemed like minutes, Mrs. Lewis came back on. Her voice seemed even colder than before. "Very well, Miss Antoine. 8:30 at the, er, pow wow grounds."

Nancy exhaled in relief. "Good. Oh, and we want the school board members there as well."

"Anything else, Miss Antoine?" the secretary asked icily.

"No. That should be fine." She hung up the phone and rushed back to the waiting students. "We've got some new planning to do," she said simply. "The meeting's on for tonight."

By 8:15 Nancy guessed that at least two hundred people had gathered at the pow wow grounds. The student teams had fanned out through the community, revisiting each house on the reserve to tell them about the meeting. Now more and more people crowded into the clearing. Roger Charlie had brought a truckload of firewood that afternoon and they had built a fire in the fire pit. The blaze crackled noisily in the centre of the circle.

Nancy watched the people. There were old women, bandannas tied around their heads. Young mothers with two or three kids in tow. Older children running and laughing, dogs barking at their heels. Men in jean jackets and worn cowboy boots. She saw George talking with a group of workers from the mill. Then, walking down the dirt road in front of the band hall, she saw a big man walking with long strides. Beside him, dwarfed by his size, was an older woman who walked with surprising spring and determination. It was her father and Mrs. Schmidt.

Nancy ran to them and hugged them both. "I didn't think you'd come," she said, smiling with delight.

"You kidding?" asked Mrs. Schmidt. "I wouldn't miss this for the world. Besides, teachers always like to see their students show what they've learned."

Just then two shiny new cars bounced along the road and pulled to a stop. Several women in high heel shoes and dresses climbed out carefully and were helped by men in suits and ties. Nancy's father reached over and squeezed her hand. "Good luck," he said.

Most of the people from the cars stood whispering together and eyeing the crowd uneasily. One man opened one of the trunks and pulled out a large flip chart. Nancy approached him.

"Mr. Dworkin?"

The man stood up and smiled. "That's right." He extended his hand. As Nancy shook it she examined the superintendent. He was younger than she'd expected, probably not more than forty-five, and he was, she conceded, quite handsome. "You must be Nancy Antoine. You have quite a crowd here. Shall we get started?"

Dworkin carried his flip chart through the crowd and set it up near the fire. Then he turned to Nancy. "Perhaps you'd like to begin?"

Nancy hesitated. She looked at the hundreds of faces in front of her and wondered if she could tell them what she felt in her heart. She began to feel some of the old fear again.

"As you know," she began, and the crowd slowly quieted. "As you know, most of the Indian students and some of the white students walked out of school three days ago. We have asked Mr. Dworkin, the superintendent, and the school board members," she waved at the men and women who had come in the cars and were now sitting uncomfortably on the grass, "to come and discuss our complaints. We hope everyone will have a chance to say what they think and," she faltered, "and maybe together we can find some solutions."

Nancy began to get over her nervousness. She glanced over at Mrs. Schmidt, who smiled encouragement. "I recently studied with one of our elders, and I came to realize that there are things we can learn, we need to learn, that your schools can't teach us." She looked at Dworkin. "There are many things to learn from the white world. We need that knowledge and those skills too. But there are also many important things that only our people, our elders, can teach us. We need to learn from each other.

"I don't have a degree from a university, but I have spent a long time in school. I know that there are ways to teach and learn that your teachers are not taught. There are goals and needs that you do not understand. There is information we need and skills that are not taught in your classrooms. And there are places to learn outside of your schools. We have to find and use them."

She stood silent and looked out at the crowd. There was a murmur that ran through the people, but she couldn't interpret it. Had she been too general? How could she explain what she felt?

Behind her Dworkin cleared his throat. "Yes, well, thank you, Nancy, and I want to assure you that we are always open to suggestions and ideas for improving our schools. However, I want to explain to you people the situation we're in. You see, our hands are really tied." His voice was reasonable, almost apologetic. He flipped to the first sheet on his chart. "You people behind me might want to shift over here so you can see this."

"Now here are the requirements for graduation that the provincial government supplies. As you can see, you must take at least eight at this level, including three here." Dworkin had a pointer he pulled out of his pocket and extended like a telescope. He stood lecturing, pointing at the graphs and diagrams, and the murmuring died down. Slowly Nancy began to see the blankness on people's faces replace the interest and excitement that had been there before. It was like watching students in a classroom, and her heart sank.

As Dworkin spoke the sun set and the sky began to turn pink. The fire seemed to brighten. Though the evening was warm Nancy shivered. She felt self-conscious in the centre, and she melted into the edges of the crowd, slumping to the grass.

"So as you can see," Dworkin finished, "we really are doing the best we can. There just isn't room for the kind of changes these students are talking about. But we know, too, that they just don't understand the intricacies and complexities of the situation. It takes those of us working in the field years and years of training, and even then" he chuckled slightly, "we don't always understand it all. So I'm sure that we can get together on this and patch up our differences."

Dworkin beamed at the crowd, and they sat silent and confused. Nancy sensed people beginning to turn away, drifting back into the growing night. A few more moments and it would be all lost. But she, too, felt subdued, too weary to speak up and try to counter the charts and numbers, the crisp logic.

Suddenly a big man pushed his way into the circle and stood

awkwardly in the firelight. Nancy realized with a start that it was her father.

He started speaking slowly. "When I was a boy..." He stopped, looked around nervously, then started again. "When I was a boy my grandfather told me a story about his father, my great-grandfather, and his vision quest." Nancy looked at the faces of the school board members sitting near her. Their expressions were mixed: annoyed, confused, patient. One man looked at the woman next to him and almost imperceptibly rolled his eyes.

"One morning while he was on his quest, he had gone out to pick berries. It was early and the mists were rising off the river. A bear, a grizzly bear, came out of the mist like a spirit. It moved slowly toward him, shuffling." Now her father moved into the centre of the circle and the fire played on his long hair and great shoulders. "He was frightened and wanted to run, but he couldn't. Slowly the big bear came toward him, sniffing the air." Her father's voice seemed to take on a growl and he swayed slightly from side to side. His shadow flickered and danced, huge and bear-like in the half-light of the fire.

"She came to him and he could see the white tips of her thick hair, the deep black of her nose, the shiny black stones of her eyes. She sniffed his hand, then gently, licked the berries from the basket he'd left on the ground. Her pink tongue lifted the red berries into her mouth."

Nancy looked at her father in astonishment. He seemed large and remote. His deep voice had become almost a chant. The red fire flickered in his eyes. As he moved around the circle, he faced the school board members, and new looks passed across their faces.

"That bear finished and walked back into the trees, but before she did she looked at my great-grandfather and told him that she would always be there to help him, to guide him, to give him strength when he needed it. And when he went to get his basket, there was a single bear's tooth lying in the bottom."

Nancy felt a shiver run up her back, and the tooth she still wore seemed to tingle against her skin.

"But you see," her father's voice seemed to soften, "I'd forgotten that story. You and your schools tore those stories out of me. You tried to kill the stories and their strength and leave me empty. And it worked too. But now I'm beginning to remember, and I won't forget again. And now some of our children are beginning to look for those stories and for that strength, and it's not in your schools. Your schools leave them feeling empty and weak, just like they did me."

The circle was hushed, and the superintendent seemed to retreat behind his flip chart as Nancy's father, large and dark in the firelight, faced him.

"Mr. Dworkin, you say you can't make room for us, our lives, our history, our stories, our future, in your schools. If that is true, Mr. Dworkin, then we have no choice but to make a school of our own."

A long silence filled the circle. Suddenly Lonnie Thomas leaped to his feet. "Now let's not be hasty," he said, smiling at the school board people. "These good people have come here to talk with us. Let's not scare them off, ha, ha, or threaten them. I mean I'm sure we can fix things up and, uh, our differences I mean ... It takes a lot of work to start a ..."

"Shut up, Lonnie," someone yelled. Lonnie's smile faded, his voice faltered, and he slipped back into the crowd.

If Dworkin had cast a spell, Nancy's father had woven a counterspell. Now Dworkin was subdued. Nancy felt the shift. She shook her head. Their own school! Of course! Why hadn't she thought of that?

Now people started to come forward. Lily Charlie began speaking in her clear, heavily accented, gentle voice.

"Oh, yes, we learned a lot in your residential schools," she said. "We learned to steal because we were always hungry. We learned to wash clothes and take orders and to be afraid of whips and straps. We came back to relatives who had never struck a child in their lives and we thought they were weak, and we disobeyed them. We learned that we were ugly. We learned to do only what we were told. We learned to despise our old ways and hate being Indian. For a hundred years, you have been telling us what we've needed to learn. And look where it's gotten us! Maybe it's time for us to decide what we need for ourselves."

Darrel Williams stood up. "And it's not so different now. I went through all your charts and I graduated. But what did I have? A lot of useless facts and no knowledge of who I was. I went to trade school, but I spent so much time trying to get myself straightened out I flunked. And now I don't fit in here either."

The rush became a torrent. People shouted out from all over the circle. "My daughter comes home from school and cries because she thinks she's stupid," someone yelled.

A mother, holding a sleeping baby on her shoulder, stood up behind Dworkin. "Your schools are not like our homes, Mr. Dworkin. We consider our children people, free to explore on their own. We don't force our kids to learn at a certain time, in a certain way. They show us what they've learned when they're ready to, not when we demand it. Our children are not used to having one person control their world. They're not used to being told what to do and how long they have to do it."

The clamor grew. Speaker after speaker talked about their anger, their frustration. Old people spoke about residential schools. "Why, do you know," one woman said, "we were even told how many squares of toilet paper we could use! Two." She raised two fingers for emphasis.

"The first time I met the brother," another related, "he pulled out a big black leather strap and told me, 'If I ever hear that you're speaking Shuswap, you'll get this over your hand.' And he did it too."

Another began. "When I went to school the brother asked me my name. 'Mouse' I said, for that was my Indian name. And that brother got the whole class to laugh at me, to ridicule me. Finally he gave me a new name. Norman."

There were younger people who talked about their school experiences. "In twelve years, I was so scared of teachers I don't think I asked a single question," one woman said quietly.

"You know I can hardly write now, and all that stuff I learned doesn't seem to have anything to do with my life," added another.

Abel Charlie spoke. "All that algebra and all, that's only any good, maybe, if you leave here. What if you want to stay? When do we learn what we can do to make this a better place?"

Dozens of people spoke and hours sped by. Nancy looked at her watch. By the firelight she could just see the hands. It was after midnight. Finally, the torrent stopped. The last speaker sat down, and the fire began to burn low in the pit. Nancy looked around. Hardly a person had left.

There was a pause that stretched for a minute, two. Then Dworkin, who had remained the whole time, wheeling to face speaker after speaker, ran his hands through his hair. He cleared his throat.

"I, I really don't know what to say," he stammered. Then he paused again. "One thing seems perfectly clear, however. We have

142

been running our schools our way, and you people have been left out." He cleared his throat again. "We have made many mistakes for you. Maybe it's time that you had a chance to make your own for a change. If you wish to start your own school, I will not oppose it."

There was a hush, then someone clapped, and then the applause tore through the crowd. People began to cheer and laugh, and Dworkin stood smiling wearily in the middle.

Somebody was shaking Nancy's hand. "It looks like we've won!"

Nancy nodded and made her way through the crowd. She found her father sitting quietly outside the circle. She rushed to him and hugged him. He started to put his big arms around her, hesitated, then clasped her close to him, laughing as she buried her face in his shoulder and wrapped her slender arms around his neck.

"I'm so proud of you, Pop," Nancy whispered. "You were great. Thanks."

Her father unlocked his arms and looked shyly at his daughter. "I felt kind of foolish at first, but then it was as if someone else was telling the story. It seemed to come from way deep inside."

Nancy hugged him again and handed him something she'd been squeezing in her fist. It was the bear's tooth hanging from the thong. It glinted red in the firelight.

"Thanks for lending this to me, Pop," she said softly, "but it belongs to you."

She took it from his hand and slipped it over his head.

XVI.

The next days were hectic. The band formed a committee to look into starting the new school and Nancy was one of the student members. At times she became exasperated and frustrated, but then the exhilaration of watching her people begin to take control of their lives overcame the fatigue, and she pushed on.

A whole new spirit seemed to surge through the community. Helplessness and apathy began to give way, and groups were forming around issues that they knew they'd ignored for far too long.

For Nancy the negotiations with Patterson were particularly satisfying. After the meeting at the pow wow grounds, there was uncertainty on both sides. The students had won the battle so far, but what happened now?

Before he left, Dworkin had told Nancy he would arrange a meeting between the students and the school staff the next day. When the time came, he met Nancy at the Corral and drove her and three other students up to the school. At first it was awkward. Patterson seemed sullen, but the teachers appeared to be more bewildered than angry.

"I didn't realize people were so unhappy," Zachary Taylor said, frowning. "You know, I think I can learn a lot from this. I'd like to discuss some of your ideas."

"Me too," Lorraine Wells agreed. "I didn't mean to bore you to death. It's just easy to, well, slip into patterns."

Bernice smiled proudly while Quigley sulked in a corner and refused to look the students in the eye.

"I don't know what's going to happen next year," Nancy explained. "But for this year I'd like an amnesty for all the students who walked out so they can return and finish off their year."

Patterson opened his mouth to object, but Dworkin motioned him to keep quiet. "I'm sure that can be arranged," Dworkin said.

The details were worked out, and Nancy found that if she came back she would probably even graduate. She told them she'd have to think about it.

When they got back to the Corral George was having a cup of coffee and waiting. Nancy sat down at the counter next to him and looked at him closely.

"Are you all right?" she asked.

"Yep. Fine."

"Why aren't you at work then?"

He turned toward her on the stool. "Quit," he said. "Yesterday."

"You quit?" she asked puzzled. "What are you going to do now?"

"I'm going away for a while."

"Away? Where to?"

"Oh, Vancouver for a start. Then I don't know. India maybe, or Guatemala. Or Peru. I don't know."

"When are you leaving?"

George drained his cup and set it down on the counter. "Today. Right now. I've got the truck packed and I'm ready to go."

"Do you think your truck'll make it to Guatemala?" she smiled.

"I'm not sure it'll make it to the highway, but I'm going to give it a try."

"Can I ride up to the junction with you?" Nancy asked.

"It's a long walk back."

"I'll manage."

They walked outside and Nancy went around to the passenger door. As she climbed in she smiled wryly at the sight of the junk that still littered the inside.

George got in and noticed her looking at the floor. "Uh yeah, well I thought about cleaning it out for the trip, but then it occurred to me that I might have to live off what I can grow, so I just threw in some more topsoil. When I get back I'm thinking about writing an article called 'The Rolling Garden — No More Eating at Truck Stops'.

They were quiet on the trip up the hill. At the top Nancy caught herself before she went for the handle, and instead reached through the window and opened the door from the outside. As she got out George turned off the motor and put the engine in gear. "No emergency brake," he explained.

He got out and walked to the front of the truck, where Nancy was standing. He leaned against the hood next to her.

"So you're really going?" she asked.

"Yeah." George looked down the highway. "I don't know. Barry's death hit me hard. I think I need to get out of here for a while." He smiled. "Maybe this will turn out to be my spirit quest."

They paused and stood quietly for a few moments.

George finally broke the silence. "So you're really staying, eh?"

Nancy smiled. "Yeah. There's so much to do here. We're

146

organizing a blockade of the railway to get them to build the walkway on the bridge. And then there's the school. We hope to have that going by the fall. There's a committee looking into forming a food co-op. Then there's the campaign to stop the logging up the Ts'elht. And this summer I want to do some more work with Mrs. Schmidt. And..."

George held up his hand, grinning. "OK, OK, you've made your point."

They stood looking at each other, their eyes warm. George held out his hands and took hers. "I've gotta go," he said softly.

"Will you come back?"

"Come back? Of course." He dropped one of her hands and pointed eastward up the river to the spot where the mountains seemed to come together and close off the canyon. He swept his arm along the tops of the peaks until he was pointing west. "This is the world. It begins here and ends there. This is my world. I'll be back some day."

Nancy squeezed his hand gently. "I'll be here," she said.